DOUBLE-CHECK
FOR SLEEPING
CHILDREN

STORIES

DOUBLE-CHECK
FOR SLEEPING
CHILDREN

KIRSTIN ALLIO

FC2
TUSCALOOSA

FC2 is an imprint of the University of Alabama Press

Inquiries about reproducing material from this work should be addressed
to the University of Alabama Press

Book Design: Publications Unit, Department of English, Illinois State
  University; Director: Steve Halle, Production Assistant: Jalissa Jones
Cover image: Stick navigation chart from the Marshall Islands;
  National Museum of Natural History, Smithsonian [E395095-0]
Typefaces: Avenir and Baskerville URW

Library of Congress Cataloging-in-Publication Data is available from
the Library of Congress.
ISBN: 978-1-57366-206-2
E-ISBN: 978-1-57366-908-5

TABLE OF CONTENTS

FOREWORD

Matt Bell

In "Ambush," the second story in *Double-Check for Sleeping Children*, Kirstin Allio's protagonist Daphne begins her tale by remembering how, as a teenager, she joined a dance class in order to "avoid having to make teenage girl conversation." Allio writes:

> That's right, avoid—my secret was that dance would exempt me from speaking altogether. I didn't understand that nobody else could really express themselves in language either. Including those smalltown girls, our dance teacher. I had no idea I wasn't alone. Stay with me as I make a leap here, in the hope of landing on a double meaning: I hadn't put it together that I wasn't alone in my body. That while I was struggling to form noes and yesses, I'd already been staked out, the culture was already speaking for me.

I'd already been staked out, the culture was already speaking for me. That sentence came back to me again and again as I read Allio's stories, many of which seem to be attempting to undo or rebut the "speaking for" that the culture wants to do on our behalf, or that parents want to do, or spouses, or men in general, or anyone else who might crowd out a character's own voice. (Or interrupt their chosen silence.) I've long believed that writing is one of the best activities for a person determined to think their own thoughts and feel their own feelings, a task that is always more complicated than it seems like it should be. But by giving close attention to the possibilities of our prose, some writers are also giving close attention to the turns of our minds and our hearts—and in my reading of these same writers, I always feel like I'm getting free of everybody else alongside them, with my freedom held aloft on the backs of their efforts.

This is all to say that Kirstin Allio's well-crafted prose demands your close attention: there is no other way to read this book but *closely*. With luck, you might find that giving these stories all the attention they require of you will also give you back more of yourself. After reading Allio's stories, you may find, as I did, that for a while your thoughts arrive in a different register, maybe even in a different time scale, as when, in the final story collected here, a chance encounter with a tortoise shifts Allio's protagonist out of human time, mother time, Anthropocene time. Suddenly, turtle time rules the clock—and afterward time does not exactly resume, but instead, as Allio describes it, *tilts*.

After certain encounters, things are forever different, and thankfully so. I can only hope that these stories leave you as time-tilted as they left me, and that they leave their mark on you in other ways too. Let me leave you with a bit of the title story of Allio's collection, wherein a character slides down a river bank on her belly "to where the stream widened and stalled into a pool," because her mother had told her, "that was the way baby bears went, and she liked to feel the heaves and rocks with her whole skin and bones." This is perhaps the best approximation I can give you of what it feels like to read Allio's fiction: if you give yourself over to her writing, you will get to experience the heaves and rocks—the sentences and the stories—not just with the mind but with the whole skin, the whole bones. What a lucky thing to find yourself holding a book like this, full of pleasures and delights and, yes, *freedoms* you can experience not just in the brain but in the body, for as long as Allio's gift of tilted time allows.

DOUBLE-CHECK
    FOR SLEEPING
CHILDREN

THE SEA

Roland Remos was fat and tall
    Off duty he wore a sun-faded baseball cap
Bottom-loaded as a mountain.
    With salt licks of sweat
He owned nine acres
    In a wave line—
Abutting his father-in-law's ninety-odd
    Never had been
Up the side of a hill
    To the sea, neither had
Long hollow from mining. Marie
    Marie, only woman he'd ever known
Was his life, county was
    Well enough to know he'd never know her
A coffee can with plenty of loose
    Besides his mother. Enough tough
Screws to cover the bottom with
    Cases out there without them
Rattling losers, miners on
    Adding their own yard of
Stamps and vets with
    Whining children.

Caved-in noses. Never took sides
    A man's heart is as big
Between townies and outlaws
    As his fist and Roland's pulse was
But he'd be lying
    Heavy, like cannons
If he said he didn't get spooked
    Underwater. He came up
Way down some cratered track, cruiser rocking
    In an apartment in town, a radio
Side to side, some private encampment with no electricity
    And a TV like a cat and dog
And no women. Like hell
    Vying for attention, but he'd learned
They wanted him nosing in on their meth
    Hunting in the forests of Proctor and Gamble
Labs, shooting ranges. He'd tried to please
    From his mother's only boyfriend—
His father-in-law
    A man a head
By moving himself and Marie out of town
    Shorter than he was. Goliath
Snowplowing his own
    Of soap don't give a shit, said Roland's mother's
Back assward mile, but
    Boyfriend, about some assholes
Her dad in his dugout
    With slingshots. You and me, son
Didn't have two words for him. Not Officer
    Capiche, Roly Poly?

Not Roland. They were men as different
　　Doesn't bother you none? Me
As a man and woman. She
　　And your old lady?
Grew corn, peas, tomatoes, he hand-
　　Roly's short neck collapsed into his fatty shoulders. Loved
Rigged a deer fence with
　　The guy like a father. He was
A volt of generator electric. She didn't like him
　　Fifteen when the guy stepped out
Shooting. She was raising
　　On them in pursuit of
A fawn indoors. Boozy, he strung a little pen—
　　Other opportunities. But by the following Indian
Boozed herself, why shouldn't she?
　　Summer, he'd slept with Marie
Didn't have to look out
　　Taught her how to read, those were the days
He liked to say, for a yard
　　Before social services. They eloped
Of spindly kids with potbellies.
　　In blue jeans, stayed drunk
He put up a tree stand
　　For a week in the woods
In princess pine where deer came
　　Like crazy Indians.
To nuzzle for drop apples.
　　With his own two hands, he built
Soft ground, an old pasture. He liked
　　Her a cabin. She'd skinned

3

To stretch out on his back
    Squirrel for her daddy, but under
On the platform, lose track of where his breath
    His roof, she'd never have
Stopped, body
    To hold a Buck knife
Started. He could sleep like a dog
    Again. He bought her a sidearm
And wake alert—
    From an officer with a sideline—
Sometimes he half dreamed she
    White water in his ears, a rush
Came to him and swept him
    When he handed her the weapon. She was still
With her hair. Then
    Slight as a girl
He'd wake ready to shoot
    Where he was a giant. When she took her afternoon
An animal. It was a blood-
    Bath, her breasts
Warm early evening
    Floated like petals
When a fawn wandered by the tree stand
    With brown, bruised centers. She was
With that way of fawns
    Whittled down from what they did
Blown, awkward,
    In the bedroom—
Ethereal. His mind
    Her stomach almost folded over

Dipped and grazed as he lay watching. If
    From the C-section, he'd seen
Only his mother could've enjoyed
    Her fight in labor, body to
These breezes. In summer a host of table fans
    Body. They were seventeen—
Shuffled hot air through the apartment. His mother
    The baby
Claimed she wore the same sack
    Already placed
Dress pregnant with him—
    For adoption. Never
Must have taken some doing
    Got her pregnant
To hold on to that dress as the fashions changed—
    Again, not after what the baby did to you.
Even a man apart, like himself, could see that
    She snorted, taking
Fawn was puny. Those weekend fat cats
    The meat off his hands. He'd stopped
From Scranton, Wilkes-Barre
    At the Quick Mart—
Would be all over these woods anyway
    She still had plenty of time
Safari time, popping off out their Jeep
    Before dinner to lie in the bath in the cabin
Windows. If he caught them at night he'd shoot out
    He built her, drink from
Their high beams. He felt
    Her private tumbler. What a life

A sealike sway as he saw
     For a woman. A couple of creatures
Marie rising
     At peace with each another for the time
From pink bathwater. He'd never told her
     Being. Hard to believe the fear
He'd pushed his way into the hospital—
     Of hunters didn't get passed down. Was that why
Stupid blindsided teenager—
     He squeezed the trigger? She threw her little pinhead up at him
He'd seen the look in the bloodshot eyes
     Looked right at him
Of his infant daughter. Already had
     Before she buckled. The air cleared. It was
A mother's fear and fury, like
     Marie's fawn. Must have
Any mother animal cut
     Got out somehow—
Off from its baby.
     A wave of sickness
Suddenly he remembered
     Remembering the time they were
His mother's boyfriend making
     Five miles deep in Proctor and
Him chase down a doe with her
     Fucking Gamble
Baby hanging out of her blasted belly—
     Dogging a doe with her
Had to wait till she dropped
     Uterus swinging between

Then wring her neck
  Her hind legs, had taken him a moment
In his own two hands. Just a moment
  To register
To register surprise at Marie's presence
  It was his own hot sobs
Before the tree stand exploded.

AMBUSH

My first dance teacher lured girls to the studio with deep conversation. Dirty secrets were cultivated and divulged—girls who danced with her were a root system of confessional alliances. Remembering it now makes it seem like a beginning. The way she seeded hints as she strode around the studio, intimations about buried shame and how it might bush, and blossom.

The studio was above the post office, although the town was a wornout patchwork of apple orchards, few addresses. Hard to imagine it needed its own zip code. The stairs from the street were pitch dark, narrow and steep as a ladder. At the top was a bathroom with a flimsy dropped ceiling where new girls took pains to change in private, and knowing girls did shots of Emergen-C to short-circuit hunger. The studio itself was big and bright, jungled with life-size houseplants. Girls on work-study soaped their giant leaves, the ritual washing of a body.

She wore parachute pants and tiny clogs—her arched feet were miniature palaces. Leg warmers and oversize rayon sweaters with the necks cut out to show her straps and pale, almost spongy shoulders. She had dog eyes and a nose job she'd gotten as a teenager. She moonlighted as a massage therapist—a table was set up behind a shoji screen in the back corner. She'd danced with City Ballet, dropped a mirror through her marble foot, lost a baby, and for reasons she never explained, had run away from the love of her life, a Black jazz dancer named Armie. She summoned him from New York or LA or Hartford several times a year for weekend intensives.

We stretched, in a circle, at the beginning of class, splayed on the hardwood floor in second position, listening to Womack & Womack, and Enya, while she paced the circle and pressed our lumbars down, bruising our tender pubes, nudging our knees with her clog to face the ceiling. Don't roll in, Daphne. Was it the pain that got girls talking? Was I the only one who was there to avoid having to make teenage girl conversation? That's right, avoid—my secret was that dance would exempt me from speaking altogether. I didn't understand that nobody else could really express themselves in language either. Including those smalltown girls, our dance teacher. I had no idea I wasn't alone. Stay with me as I make a leap here, in the hope of landing on a double meaning: I hadn't put it together that I wasn't alone in my body. That while I was struggling to form noes and yesses, I'd already been staked out, the culture was already speaking for me.

My mother got my name, Daphne, from the myth where a girl becomes a tree to escape Apollo's predations. It made perfect sense, as if my fate were to be mute, disguised by leaves and bark, rooted. But then I shocked everyone and uprooted, mid high school, straight to New York City. A touristy T-shirt from the era, sold on the street, worn by no self-respecting dancer but purchased furtively by many transplants, me included, depicted two robo-primitive figures, a white dancer on black background and a Black dancer on white background, a sort of jagged, yin-yang graphic, flinging their limbs at the same bongo. Keith Haring's *Dance or Die New York City*. I loved music, I loved dance, I loved training. It was incredible to track yourself for hours a day as if from the outside, by which I mean mirror training—as if through others' eyes. It was training for empathy, and dissociation.

Were you good at dancing? my kids used to ask me. As if on cue, my sternum lifted. Sometimes I'd say, I was tall. And they'd stamp their little feet in frustration. They were tired of hearing that they were going to be tall too. For a long time, I thought that was all that was left of it.

*

It was the week between Christmas and New Year's. Penny was home from school, blaming us for her regression, and Ethan was rummaging for leftovers with less and less optimism. I guess I'm going to have to start drinking, Ed warned us on the depressing morning of the twenty-eighth, lunging into the liquor cabinet. He came out with a bottle of gin someone had given us twenty years ago as a housewarming present, regarded it with bewilderment.

This was the mood in which he yearly campaigned for a road trip. Where would we go? I countered weakly. Because despite the malaise of the household, the sink despondent with dishes, I never really wanted to go anywhere. And due, perhaps, to the symbiosis of mothers and children, even nearly grown ones, Penny and Ethan weren't exactly clamoring for an adventure either.

Abandoning the gin, Ed cried, I'm taking you to Paris!

I retreated to our bedroom. I was reading a new collection of Zadie Smith stories, courtesy of Penny. She had watched me with such unreserved anticipation as I slipped the ribbons down the shoulders of the package, sliced the seam of wrapping paper. Ooh, Penny!

I'd read everything since *White Teeth*.

But in fact I felt traitorous handling the handsome hardcover. How could Penny know I didn't read Zadie Smith because I loved the novels? Or, I loved them because I imagined Zadie and myself as contemporaries. Becuase I was all stirred up that a girl my age could have such a big voice, authoritative bearing. Thank you, Sweetheart, I'd said. Do you want to take it back to school with you when I'm finished? She waved me off, and I thought how at her age, twenty-one, I was still crossing the floor in chaînés turns, footless pink tights and black leotard.

She hung now in my bedroom doorway, twisting to crack her back. I'd been unable to convince her it was a disgusting habit. How's it going? she said. I stopped myself from remarking that her teeth were yellow. Instead: I'm not sure yet. She perked up. Did you check out any of the reviews? She never thought I was qualified to make judgments. You would have loved college, she was fond of saying. I knew she thought she sounded supportive. I waited for her to pad off again. I couldn't tell her I thrilled defiantly to Zadie as "a coworker in the mother trade—a topnotch craftsman." It was a line from Grace Paley I'd loved forever. But then, of course, who was I kidding? Look how Ed was made forcefully rich off the Internet, off the raw material of human want, weakness, and boredom. Look how all the while I raised exemplary children, kept the home fires burning, oftentimes by organizing takeout. My comrades, mothers-in-arms, were ladies who picked at leaf-based lunches.

I rolled off my couch and ventured downstairs quietly. I didn't want anyone to get the idea I was available. Ed had gone outside to vacuum his car as if he might actually take off somewhere without us, but I saw out the kitchen windows that he was shooting hoops with our eight-year-old next-door neighbor.

Ethan had given me *God Is Not Great*, by Christopher Hitchens, as if he'd written it himself, and so both kids chose British authors, and Ed and I had presented them with fat checks inside scrawled cards—Xmas wishes!—signaling our defeat in knowing what they wanted.

So no Paris, said Ed. But we could drive a mere two hours and be in the Berkshires. For some reason, I remembered how in the summer of 1998, before we were married, Ed had pressed his cell phone upon me when I went away for the weekend. I'd been charmed and flustered and worried about the rate per minute. Was I only to use it to call Ed, who would answer the landline in his apartment? Hard to know what the equivalent gesture would be in today's socioromantic currency. But the memory provided the logic of relenting, and as December twenty-ninth dawned monochrome and migraine-y, out came our soft-bodied rolling suitcases, and while Ed shot like an arrow, I was a quiver, deer skin, dangling beads, some of them missing, dark inside a leather pouch, and I felt I had no idea where I was going. In fact, I realized that leaving the house now caused me a kind of territorial anxiety, as if I no longer knew who I was without a daily point of origin, and as if in drift, danger, or even death would find me easy to ambush.

Penny and Ethan were sluggish but not wholly recalcitrant. There was something frivolous about the way they didn't seem to know how to pack, and became suddenly, helplessly, hungry. Despite their Milk-Bone height and heft, they might as well have fit into the palms of our hands.

Ed drove us out the back of our city, away from the ocean, which meant bankrupt drive-ins, their dead screens looming over the tree line, and the abandoned outposts of off-brand gas stations. Crossing the state line into Massachusetts, we wound past collapsed motels and skeleton lodges with the wind blowing straight through them.

Don't stare, Ethan, said Penny. Don't talk to me like that, said Ethan with good humor. I should have been immune to the startling visuals. The fire-stained pile of stones, half-buried camper that marked our turnoff marked my childhood. At least I shouldn't have been a voyeur. A nest of old cars had dragged themselves to die on the compound up the road, in the floodplain of a vociferous little mountain river. Our closest neighbor was holed up under a fluorescent tube in his ancestors' unheated farmhouse, surrounded by decommissioned apple orchards, infested with poison ivy and hunters in all seasons, whose dogs would scent me, howling, and pin me against a raggy apple tree until the hunters themselves approached, leering. No wonder I fled to the city.

In the final stretch of the outer Berkshires, we plunged and curved into a wintry canyon occupied with quiet scintillation by an ice storm.

We arrived after lunch at the motel in North Adams. There was a handsome fire in the lodge, and in the rooms, pine-scented soap, and stacks of reproductions of spent postcards with color-tinted scenery. Cool handwriting, said Ethan. It felt conspicuous, suddenly, that we had come to see art. Come to gape at the repurposing of a postproductive white poverty town—with just the right seams still showing. I was wearing oversize carpenter's jeans and a shrunken, chunky black wool sweater. Penny was in an air hostess dress circa 1970.

Even Ed admitted he was slightly nauseated from travel, but in pursuit of fresh air we'd scope out the scene for tomorrow's visit. We followed the Hoosic River past the original worker row houses and came in view of the former Sprague Electric—hundreds of thousands of square feet of vintage red brick transformed into the museum industrial complex, I spouted.

Good one, said Ethan. Courtesy of the Canadian who coined "the media is the message," I continued, or is it medium, I added, and Penny sniggered. I don't want to know, I said defiantly. Single-handedly would I defy the extinction of questions due to the Internet.

Oh, Mother, sighed Penny.

We went with pizza for dinner. Ethan pried off the lid, then dumped out the entire shaker of yellowed parmesan. He added red pepper flakes as if he hoped they were a food group. An older couple along the cinder-block wall were shapeless, stoically abstract in their hooded sweatshirts. There was some sense of droit du seigneur, I thought, as if we were invited to make the locals part of our art experience. At the same time, we were invisible to them, the way the ruling class always perceives itself omniscient. Certainly, the Stonehenges—hoods up, enduring—were authentic. The art in the museum, however—could the conceptual be authentic? Certainly it could be clever. It could spurn our overtures of interpretation. At the same time, it would most definitely have an agenda, an axe to grind, and I found I was prepared to feel coerced by its terms and conditions. It was the kind of art that didn't work without a tricky cultural consensus. Without the reading of a narrow set of publications.

I was picking off my green peppers and black olives. How strange, I thought, that I loved this kind of art as I once loved dance, beyond reason.

We were ready for the museum in the morning. The space was vaulted darkly like a cathedral, and I found myself effortlessly transported. This was the grandeur of the calling, I thought, and even though I'd given up dancing in defeat, I felt the power of having once been inducted. If not ultimately chosen, at least I'd been allowed to burn for a while.

The headliner exhibit had a song lyric for a title. I did an embarrassing little head fake as I took over the lines, feeling suddenly loose and dance-y, extending Kanye's urgent delivery—*That shit cray*, I whispered, moving my long wool coat to my forearm. At the threshold of a great hall of worn brick and striated concrete, I could almost hear the music coming in over the PA system. Hype, anthemic. It went right to my heartbeat.

I regarded a crack the length of an entire wall. It was certainly art in that it held meaning. There was a waxy, creepily confessing Punch, from Punch and Judy. A painting of stacked rows of molars was surreal, childlike—anxious-making. *Suffering from Realness*. A worshipful hush pervaded. Was this, in fact, the sacred space where questions could hang unanswered, impervious to reality, and the Internet? I thought I knew what Kanye meant by suffering from realness, that all of fame's phantasmagoria couldn't take away the truth of the human condition. But then I was spinning it—if realness was truth, then suffering from realness meant suffering due to the loss of truth, which was really the loss of innocence, the way we used to assume we were generally agreed with, the way we still think we're right, just blindsided now by the fact that other people think they're right, too—Almost as soon as the thought completed, I realized I'd made a leap in the wrong direction. Of course I wanted to align myself with the artist, the sufferer. That was how art worked, wasn't it? But my rightness was the realness of others' suffering. I might have been spinning it, but it was my own head that was spinning.

I saw Ed's long form in the distance. I clung to the truth that my feet hurt, that the ball mound of my right big toe was killing me even though I was wearing new sneakers.

We waved to each other. He was faster through a museum than I was. He would be formulating art questions for the kids, who would be girding for them, but generous. We were known, I thought, as a close family, by the kinds of families who would say such a thing after staring too long at the way we joked around. I always thought they were angling for a reciprocal compliment, but Ed was sure it was a benediction.

*

Penny had gone straight back to her old yoga studio when she got home for Christmas. She wanted me to come to class, proposing as she sidled up to me, My treat? which made us laugh, like equals. Despite having been a dancer, or maybe because of it, I'd always believed I hated yoga, its pious unmusicality, agonizing slowness, and the only other time I'd gone was when she was in high school, feeling protective of her, and maybe a little bit jealous of her favorite teacher. I'd ended up waiting the entire class out in child's pose, inarticulately offended. This time, Penny rented a mat for me almost proprietarily. She grabbed the right props, set them up just so, and I felt that she placed our mats demonstratively close, signaling to all the other acolytes that she and I were together. I felt a rush of devotion to my daughter as if I were a new wife, fresh from the altar.

I'm so tight, she whispered, upside down. She was bouncing in downward-facing dog, threatening to kick up into a handstand. The heat in the studio was coming at me in waves. My feet and my palms were already sweating. You'll be great, Mom, she said as she landed lightly.

Was it the heat, in fact, that expanded my vision? My history came to me as a geological record, all the bodies I'd ever been in layers in different colors, waiting to be recognized. Float your eyes, cascade your tail. I had danced to circumvent speech, but how had I forgotten about the metaphors, the body language of a dance class? Sharpen your elbows, recruit your abdominals! I slipped out of the studio. The front-desk girl in sheepskin slippers was playing a private little movie on her phone. I am so sorry to bother you, I said, but may I borrow a pen and paper?

Had to pee? said Penny afterward. I started to explain, but then she was introducing me to her goddess, Ravenna, who was not much older than Penny herself, narrow hipped, febrile, beautiful except for a skin condition that looked like overtanned acne.

I loved the language, I started, but Ravenna was complimenting me blandly on being Penny's mother. I have a son too, I said, and she flashed her teeth. She had pomegranate-painted nails. But he can't touch his toes, I continued stupidly, and Ravenna looked straight through me, so that I felt even stupider, step-ball-change, like I was the chimp and Penny the long-suffering primate scientist.

*

We decided to have a picnic dinner in our room, Ed's and mine, with groceries from Price Chopper. We had to run across four lanes from the motel to the shopping plaza, as headlights starburst upon us. I almost lost my balance, but Penny hauled me onward. It had seemed ridiculous to get in the cold car just to cross the highway.

Penny and I stood blinded at the mile-long row of registers. Ethan was already hugging a bag of potato chips like a space suit. Oranges, said Penny, determining our course. Slim pickings, I added, as we narrowed in on hummus in a tub, a mixed package of carrots and celery. Ethan could palm eight yogurt cups. He was six-foot-five and did not play basketball. What would Dad like? I said, and Ethan eyed some quiches hopefully. Those will be vile, said Penny. The choices, she declared, aren't killing it.

But in fact, my heart had steadied, and I realized that my happiness was uncompromised. Let's check out every aisle, I said, then we can say we checked out every aisle. The kids laughed together. Prunes? Peanut butter? We remembered we needed drinks, we stumbled into the decorator alcove of gourmet cheeses and Finnish rye crisps, ageless biscotti.

Crossing the highway back to the motel, the kids insisted on carrying the bags, leaving me with an strange new lightness.

The next morning, we reconvened in the motel lodge for the roaring fire, the free coffee, the ritual jokes about Ethan stunting his growth, and the free refills. Who vacations in North Adams in late December? We had the place to ourselves. The staff were young and white—Surly, said Ed, and I said, I don't know about that. Just inattentive. I had brought the oranges from last night's supermarket run, and we peeled them all over the table. Ed spied yesterday's *New York Times*, poorly refolded, possibly unsanitary, and it was more about Trump's white Right, the pitchfork crowd that wanted time to somehow shrug itself backward, and the white Left, I said self-consciously, who regarded the past, present, and future as one temporal and moral territory. Presentism. What? said Ed. That's the term for it. That your past is the same as your present, I said, and should be served up to your future. What makes you think you can turn on your own kind? Ed said playfully.

Ethan was staring out the window as if even his gaze were longer than that of a normal-height human. Both kids had tuned out and it seemed suddenly artificial for Ed and me to be having this conversation without them. I looked at him directly and tried to transmit this, and he looked back at me and shrugged to signal understanding and agreement. Does anyone recall who it was who said that intelligence is the ability to hold conflicting thoughts at once? he asked the table.

Do you mean what great man? said Penny, idly, from her planet. Preach, Penelope, said Ethan. It was the kind of thing I never knew or could not remember. But conflicting thoughts at once—thoughts that canceled each other out, leaving me thoughtless, speechless—that was my specialty. I'd never been able to protect a single certainty. I'd danced to avoid speaking, which was antithetical to the kind of male intelligence we were talking about, and even my own daughter was sort of masculine, in the way that all Internet children were protomen, DNA-ed by the greats of Microsoft, Google, Apple—I was off again—and when I looked up they'd switched to the sports section, which they were all reading and relishing together, even Ethan, who'd done gymnastics, capoeira, tae kwon do, fencing, parkour, and geocaching, all in order to avoid teams, and who was just now parodying happily, The humanity, Dad! The heroism!

By the time we finished breakfast it was midday. In full sunlight, nature looked more iconic than impoverished, and we decided to skip the museum and go hiking.

It turned out the motel backed up onto the Appalachian Trail. The property included an overdesigned bridge suspended almost comically high above a juvenile river. A solitary duck drew the current like a cloak behind it, and as we bounced across, Ethan wondered if the tributary was a tribute to the mighty Hoosic. Ha ha, said Penny. Ed had to say, Hoosic, who's sick? Ha ha, said Ethan. We'd borrowed the forest-green Baedeker-style trail map available at the front desk, and we identified the landmarks: a yoga platform; a couple of nominally interactive wind chimes, or rather, "sound sculptures." The ambient whine of a chainsaw, the road's slightly hollow thunder—there was still snow splayed across the path in the shade, ice under the mud, and I regretted wearing sneakers.

We crested the motel property on a higher road cut into the mountainside. We walked single file along the salted shoulder, cars and trucks practically exploding alongside us with boomerang gusts of wind. We had to squeeze ourselves into the brush when we met a group of hen-like girls coming the other way, smoking, bellies bare, impervious to the cold. Ed was the only one of us who deigned to say hello to them.

Soon, as the map foretold, there was the notably retiring sign for the Appalachian Trail, and we headed up a dirt road that doubled as someone's driveway, a moaning pine tree in the front yard. I felt the old childhood fear of trespassing, being caught on someone else's land—my parents had been thrifty, self-taught homesteaders, but not natives. But this forest was positively inviting. Soon we were winding up alongside a wide, rocky stream, glaucous with ice at the edges, and we paused to watch how it flushed fast and clear down the middle. The highway noise seemed to have been turned off, said

Ethan, and we all cocked our ears. I felt the flow of us, settling into rhythm, and despite what I said before about the kids not being self-reliant, the way they couldn't seem to count their socks and underwear, it was true that each adult and semiadult was now, at last, responsible for his or her own body. I kept thinking, in these exact words, This must be good for everyone's soul, and, Look what a good mother, what a wife, what a giver of mountains I am.

There was the luxury now, of not always talking, like we'd had to do through their childhoods, as if we were their lifelines. How I used to long to get lost in a side thought. But now, suddenly, I felt myself a little withdrawn, even mournful, in the silence. Penny had caught me in my room on her first night home and quietly closed the door: Ethan seems so good, she'd whispered, fiddling with the angle of my reading lamp intensely. Well, I said, he is seventeen. Penny said, That's insane. Thanks to a ton of pills and a ton of tutors, right, Mom? I looked up ahead to his hulking form on the trail now. Where did he find all that material to grow with? Light and soil? He was more like a horse than a tree. He still didn't have what I would call a real friend. He didn't know how to share power. His teachers thought he was a cheater for years, when all the while he was a strategist. I suspected he still carried the harm of being falsely accused.

I remembered walking him back from the orthodontist against a bustling spring wind, stopping to sit on a low, sun-stung wall on busy Waterman Street. Was it only last year? He didn't need me to accompany him anymore, but it was so long-standing, this ritual of ours, and there was something wonderfully illicit about meeting him in the middle of his school day.

He'd wanted to postpone returning to class, he hated English, and, No wonder, I exclaimed when he said they were reading David Foster Wallace. Ethan looked at me sideways. He was cantilevered over his knees. He said in teacher falsetto, Now who ushered in the New Sincerity, Ethan? Ermmm, he fake-stammered. Methinks—he cut his eyes at me slyly. But actually, he said, what's wrong with David Foster Wallace? Wasn't he, like a prodigy at tennis?

Oh, gosh, I laughed. He probably thought girls couldn't play.

One of the old dead white dudes, said Ethan. He put his head down on his forearms. He really was like a horse, the way he had to sink and crane to your level to hear, the way he watched the world out of the corners of his eyes. He was off his meds at long last, but he had been granted extended time, which sounded either poetic or bureaucratic, and effectively allowed him to lap his classmates. Ed said, Are you shitting me? How does that help him become a man? But neither of us had the courage to revoke a superpower. With twice the time to fill in the bubbles, he'd gotten perfect scores on his SATs.

Ethan and I sat there on the wall in silence for a while. I realized I was staring at the cryptic stickers on the back of a stop sign. Globalism Is Rape Culture. It seemed like the Nextel chirp was everywhere. Cars scored the air and then the air sealed behind them. The sun suddenly turned an unreadable gray, like a screen, and I said, Why don't you just come home?

New Sincerity. Postmodernism. I wouldn't have lasted a minute in college. There might be an emerging state of being you could call postdepression, though. Knowingness and connection, I thought now, although not in any positive way—just a deep cognition of the end of world. How we're all going down together, the skeeters and the squirrels, avuncular Warren Buffett, Uber drivers and pole dancers and shack dwellers in the Berkshires, their shacks too, hanging on by their horned toenails, even the mountain is going down.

Dark fell early, especially on the east-facing, wooded trail, leaving the impression that the planet was wreathed in gravity. It was barely past three. The temperature dropped, and it was clearly time to turn around. In fact, it felt like a roof was being drawn, and I remembered how sleep, last night, had felt like a roof, with an extra lorazepam.

We separated into two groups, as I was slipping badly in my sneakers, in contrast to Penny and Ethan, who had all their knees. Ed and I followed their footprints in the snow. They had been known to run down mountains. It's nice we don't have to be the intermediary anymore, I said.

Ed made a scoffing sound, They're probably plotting against us. I couldn't imagine it but I laughed. See, Daph? said Ed gently if opportunistically. You can leave the house every once in a while.

We came out of the woods and the sky seemed to cling. There was a strong smell of sulfur, and the kids were waiting for us under the pine tree, looking orphaned. What is that smell? said Ethan, as if betrayed. That, said Ed, is the smell of sin. Once again, we organized ourselves single file on the highway shoulder. We passed an aluminum-and-plastic dwelling that was sending out rolls of smoke. Sirens in the distance—we covered our mouths and noses with our hands.

Ed and Penny got ahead and Ethan reined himself in to stay with me, seeing, I suspected, an opening to petition for drivers education. We'd tied it to grades, although such a tactic was considered retro parenting; really, we were just trying to buy some time for the frontal lobe. I'd logged my driver's ed hours with Fran LaFrenier, a Catholic bachelor with a snow-white helmet of hair and a monopoly on generations of student drivers. I told Ethan he liked to brag about how many of his students had been killed on the road. How many? Ethan rallied. Now that I think of it, I said, he was the henchman of the god of the underworld. Sheesh, said Ethan. My license was conditioned on mastery of the oil change. My dad was most likely the only guy in town who paid at the recycling center to dump his used oil, and he did so religiously, and I'd go along for a chance to forage in the clothes bins. People were throwing their TVs away before we'd gotten our first one, he used to say like a mantra, with stars in his eyes.

I looked up at Ethan's long face, Do you know what a dipstick is?

He said, Is that a real question? But I could sense he was going to let me run on for a while. He was happy walking, not making eye contact, listening to the whir of my voice, never mind the words.

We possessed an ancient Saab that rolled backward down hills instead of climbing them. The ignition was between the seats and it collected lint like a naval. It had almost two hundred thousand miles by the time I got the keys, but it was impossible to walk alone on the backweave of dirt roads. Impossible to walk alone on the highway. Wanna ride? From the time I was ten years old, Wanna get laid? How did I allow myself to get caught again and again? It wasn't being alone that scared me, but being discovered alone—that brought me shame.

A car passed so close now it sprayed us with surface gravel. I wish we had something reflective, I said, and Ethan picked up his huge shoe and showed me where it shone.

We turned down the hill onto the motel property. By the time we reached the suspension bridge, we were far behind Ed and Penny. We paused before crossing. Do you want to go a little farther? I asked. Ed would be happy on vacation to kick back and watch premium TV, and Penny had a gift for taking beatific naps before dinner, but Ethan and I shared a physical restlessness, a proclivity for light exploration. Let's do it, Mom, said Ethan. We stood for a moment evaluating the crossroads. It didn't matter that we both knew there was just more scrub forest giving on to bleak, salt-measled rural roads. Then I felt a presence. My scalp tightened. A man was headed our way on the main riverside trail. My back was slick with sudden sweat, as if fear were a kind of exertion. He was a little guy, as Ed would say, in bulky clothes, work boots, wearing a backpack. But not a hiker. The path was flat and straight, and my view as he got closer was unimpeded. I could see his smoker's skin, white-blue eyes, and what looked to be a military-grade bow and arrow sticking out of his backpack.

He slowed when he reached us. Static plowed into my ears. My long arms would soon begin waving like tethered branches. The hunter took a step closer and looked straight into my eyes, the way we'd both been trained. My fear was his prize, and as he absorbed it, his chest filled. From far away I heard Ethan say, Hey, man.

Calculations prickled to life as my blood resumed flowing. Angles of escape, relativity to safety. But I knew not to turn and look after him. Like with dogs, not to incite, excite them. I said, Is he gone?

Who? Ethan said.

Are you serious?

That dude?

I looked at the swaying bridge, and I said, I'm not sure I can cross that crazy bridge, Ethan.

You can do it, Mom.

I walked him to his and Penny's room. We took turns struggling with the door—there was no handle, just raw wood flush with stylish raw-wood cladding—and it was thick, like the door of a bank vault, and I thought Ethan might actually bend the key in the lock forcing it. I poked my head in after him. Penny was in dreamland.

There was a stain in the sky as if the sun had left rust where it rested, and the melted snow had iced over. The property was designed with ironic homage to the roadside motel it once was, with rows of units squared to make a commons. The website showed a meadow in the summer, maybe an acre, inclined toward the river and scattered with delicate, young birch trees like penned antelope. It was a tundra now. Heading out, I lost my footing over bunched grass trapped in a mound of buttered snow. I was still shaken. Ed's and my room was on the far side of the property. I slipped again, to my knees this time. Rookie mistake, hiking in sneakers. At least no one had seen me. The tundra wasn't a fishbowl.

But just then, again—a presence, and there he was, the bowman, sighting me deftly from across the field. He was on the service path behind the buildings, where the maids parked carts of linens and the Big Gulps they nursed all day. He must have tracked me from the road. He saw me see him and he raised his chin. One end of the bow stuck up behind him, an exposed wing bone.

My trajectory was on a diagonal, and he was moving down toward the river. I understood that our paths would converge when I reached the lower corner of the square, on his side, at the door to my room, which was impossible to open, the same as the kids' door.

Don't be crazy, I thought. You're an old lady. I hated my fear, my imagination. I saw myself through his eyes. His dance partner. How much time did I have? The terrain organized itself once more into escape angles, but I couldn't run on the ice and snow and I saw myself from far away—too far to rescue.

As I moved, he popped up again in the next opening between buildings. Loose and dance-y. My steps, in contrast, were small and stiff, as if I were hobbled, and I was barely making progress. You're a big girl now, said a voice. It was my voice. I wondered if I were dreaming, and as if in a dream, I thought that if I screamed, no one would hear me.

He disappeared behind the last building, then came out inside the commons. He beckoned me toward him. I heard that voice again, my own, Time to get moving. And I found myself turning lightly and heading back up the hill toward the lodge, and the road, not looking back, keeping my eyes trained on the dimming sky.

There was a groundskeeper in a denim onesie and I quietly entered his orbit. Hi, I heard myself say, surprisingly natural.

He looked surprised to see me. Can I help you? My face must have been visibly shimmering. Sorry, I said, I'm a little shaken. He cocked his head. Just then a helicopter roared up the sky and he raised his eyes behind thick, desk-job glasses. I might have picked somebody up in the woods, I said. I'm so sorry. I knocked my fist against my breast as if to reset the controls. I could see that he neither liked nor believed me, and while I understood that embarrassment was a kind of self-sabotage, even debasement, I heard myself stutter, This actually isn't like me at all, I'm so embarrassed. I laughed hectically.

Why don't you tell me what seems to be the problem?

I said we'd met a guy on the other side of the suspension bridge, I said I'd noticed the bow and arrow, that I grew up with hunting, it wasn't that, and I totally got how this could be perceived, and then I'd thought we'd lost him, but he followed us out after all—I dropped my son off—I was trying to get to my room—

He raised his arm and I stopped accordingly. He was pointing at another groundskeeper, same uniform, but older and seedier looking. In a perfectly normal voice he asked me, Was it him?

No, no, I laughed, and I understood that he was entitled to a little fun now, trying to trick me into making a false accusation.

Was it him? said the groundskeeper in the same exact voice, pointing again, to an overbuilt guy in a black sweater and a black, motel-merchandise watch cap.

No, I said. I thought, how did I get here?

He said solemnly, You say a bow and arrow?

I'm familiar with hunting, I pleaded—Well, he cut me off then, the only thing you really have to worry about around here are the mighty MAGAs. So, you okay now?

All I wanted was for him to walk me across the tundra to the door of my room, and to wait while I stabbed the key in the gritty lock, and to stand guard while I threw my shoulder at the vault-slab of wood swollen in the frame.

I'm just going to sit in the lodge for a while, I managed, and he shrugged, and we parted.

There was no one else in the common area. The fire was crackling and I went up close and stuck my hands out in front of it. My face was burning. I was hot with shame. But all at once it froze me, that phrase, for suddenly I heard it different-ly. Hot with shame. Does shame make women hot? Was that the message, the real meaning?

My first dance teacher—it's hard not to see a ballet mistress as a kind of madam. At least a broker of initiation. I closed my eyes. I saw her trailing wilted costumes, trying to impart to us that life really was like the myths behind the great ballets. We were all prey and predators. Go forth, girls. Break the spell, or just run while you still can.

DOUBLE-CHECK FOR SLEEPING CHILDREN

Down the bank on her belly, to where the stream widened and stalled into a pool. Her mother said that was the way baby bears went, and she liked to feel the heaves and rocks with her whole skin and bones.

Where the hell did you come from? said a voice.

She pointed up the bank before she located him, full camo, half tree—

Well come on down, he said reasonably.

She slipped the rest of the way.

Are you my father? she asked.

He laughed. You ain't got one of your own?

He added after a while, You ask your ma? When she didn't answer, the fisherman looked up through the bare trees to find his laugh again. Got me a granddaughter.

Hannah said quickly, My age?

Yes, ma'am.

Now she tried to contain her voice to hide her eagerness to know, How old would that be?

Bout five.

All right. They were getting to know each other and he handed her the rod. You're a natural, he said, admiring the way she took hold. He stepped back a good way to let her get a feel, and that was lucky, she thought, because all at once the fishing rod came alive. She felt a tug down deep to her source, like the stream was inside.

From far away she heard him, You Lady Luck, little girl?

She knew what she was. She closed her eyes. But then he was behind her, heavy and strong, knocking the magic pole away. Her eyes flew open and he caught her midair—

The fish was already going still between his hands.

She had the sense to scatter a different way from how she'd found the stream. That fisherman with his face twitching like last fall's beech leaves would never know where she and her mother stayed. They made a brush bed in darkness that cats have golden eyes for, that deer have rabbit's-foot-for-luck tails for. Her mother buried her nose in Hannah's hair at night and Hannah held still as if she were her mother's prey. Her mother said, You're playing dead on me. Later Hannah caught a whiff of sulfur shit from the hole her mother dug with her spade.

They were on the move. They were staying out of the way of a man. I'm speaking in code, comrade, said her mother, and her look grew both larger and blurrier by the fire. Is he a fisherman? Hannah asked.

Why? Her mother seemed to contract inside her skin.

It was hot for early spring, and the bare, pronged woods were overexposed, said her mother ominously, extraterrestrial. *Home, home on the range*, her mother had a real singing voice, and she beat time out the window against the side of the car, so that the car was filled with wind, *Where the deer and the antelope play.* She doubled back on the same fragment of tune, *Heading east out of western PA . . .*

They were on a long, straight section of road when Hannah looked around behind them to see a river shimmering on their tail.

When the pioneers crossed the country in covered wagons, said her mother, squinting as if to conjure the indomitable line of a caravan, they had visions of lagoons, lakes, willow trees.

Hannah looked around again and reported back, Police cars. Her mother raised her eyes quickly to the mirror. She started to draw her arm in the window, then she hung it back out again. She added, They were too stupid to ask the Indians where the water was. And she gave her daughter the same wide, blank smile she used at filling stations when she turned out her pockets, having already pumped a full tank of gas.

There was a well-kept double-wide with cars pulled up all over the lawn and filed along the side of the road. A flag flew from the mailbox, and Hannah's mother slowed the car. As she pulled over Hannah saw her take in the not-so-distant crossroads.

Hannah leapt out and made for a life-size, white-furred bear with a wink in his last glass eye. When she remembered it later, the scene, and the things she chose—a stripy hula hoop, a pair of pink plastic clogs, Nancy Drew with tidy calves and low heels, bearing a lantern against the opening of a sinister cave—she wondered how she knew it was a yard sale. It was strange the way you remembered surprise, but couldn't quite replay your own innocence.

A tall girl with bangs in her eyes was picking her way toward them. A boy shot from behind the garage to gyrate at the edge of the yard as three police cars tooled by. Hannah's mother waved to the older girl. Are you taking paper dollars here? Valerie—Hannah would soon learn her name—looked confused, but curious. In a flash, Hannah saw her mother through Valerie's eyes: rouged with road dirt, a braid the girth of her fist that Hannah herself had never seen undone. Hannah stepped between them, but her mother was already engrossed, foraging in her blanket coat, its deep folds. Bowing like a foreign emissary in her thigh-high moccasins and holding forth a bill, she said, That should do the trick, comrade. She reached for Hannah's shoulder and then bowed again as if to excuse herself, saying to Hannah, Go on. Hannah set out after Valerie, toward the kicked-open kitchen door.

The house was dark and cool. Pretty women sat at the kitchen table smoking and drinking canned sodas, and they swiveled as one to see the girls.

Hi! cried Valerie's mother. She looked older than Hannah's mother. Curly blond hair. Her whole chin smiled and she had big, friendly ears. Gentle eyes. As she touched Valerie's old things with her polished shells, their worth multiplied.

How old are you? asked one of the women from the table, afloat in an off-the-shoulder ruffle, blowing smoke out of the way. Before Hannah could answer, Valerie's mother said, I bet you're in first grade.

I've never been to school, said Hannah, and the women froze. I like your rabbits, she said, trying to find favor again. There were china animals in tea parties and parades, and the women all laughed and stubbed out their cigarettes and reached for their cans. Valerie's mother was doing the math on the cover of the phone book.

I'll help you carry your stuff, said Valerie, and Hannah knew Valerie wanted to get another look at her mother's curled lip, animal flinch, wild eyes.

Someone called, Come back soon!

Hannah's arms barely reached around the polar bear. In the bright sun, she was momentarily blind. Valerie pranced off the asphalt to the lawn. Bare feet, she said. Ow. Where's your mom? Where's your car? she said, surprised, setting the bags down.

That was how Hannah was left the first time. In her mind's eye, she saw the car burst free.

Time lifts off here. Lost, lofts along before it grounds again.

Ten years passed, and when her mother returned, Hannah was almost sixteen. She didn't want to leave Valerie, Amy her foster mom, get back on the road.

But her mother seemed overcome by the sight of her. Forgive me, she said, in a voice twisted and wrung out like a rag, lowering herself to one knee.

*

The Shell was awash, everything melting sideways. A shining black lake of asphalt. What they used to do in high school, thought Martin Grenier, was get somebody with four-wheel drive to haul them up the old state logging road to the top of the quarry, then they'd fake death out by walking straight off the ledge. That deep blade of water three stories below.

Remembering it got to his bowels. If he needed another sign of getting old.

Terry Jarnot, speaking of high school, pulled up on the other side of the pumps, and Martin could see the dog in profile, riding high.

By way of greeting, Isn't that your place out by me? said Jarnot. One of your rentals? he added, as if it were a cathouse, or Martin some kind of overlord.

Martin felt a twinge in his side; they'd pushed the hernia back in the hole, the problem was with his own scar tissue tugging at the stitches now.

Jarnot's eyes were locked on the counter, the dollars racing ahead of the gallons these days. Martin too felt duped by the price of gas, driving between properties all day and all he ever did was fill the truck, forty, fifty bucks used to be something big you made a decision on.

Been quiet out there for a week, said Jarnot, building his case. Maybe two.

But what, pussy around in one of those Al Gore-mobiles? A fool with bald eyes like a bird. Martin's daughter, Jessica, she was a heavy breather when it came to what they were calling the climate. Jessica at the stove—turkey bacon from here on out, said the colorectal doctor. A heart attack of love when Jessie set down the plate of facon. The way she came over and took charge.

Jarnot got back in his truck with that shotgun dog. Had a beak just like its owner. Okay guy. Nice to meet somebody you

know from time to time, anyway, Martin was thinking when
Jarnot pointed his elbow out the window and said, The lady
took off. The girl was there by herself for a while, kept my eye
out, but now she's gone too.

Well, he'd better get over there and see. Past Jarnot's place
on the corner and coasted to the end of the cul-de-sac. Scrub
woods, the developers had backed out after he made the first
move, him trying to show Sue, sure, impress his wife with what
they were calling his risk profile. One look now he knew his
tenants had gone AWOL. Which surprised him, being females
that walked off, in this case that gal renter was too skinny to
be well, and the teen daughter. Pretty girl. Gal paid in cash
and he couldn't come up with her name now. Had this drama
about her, almost church, when she said, This is my daughter Hannah. We're reunited now. What was that supposed to
mean?

Where you from? he'd asked.

We're making our home here.

Jessica said he was in the vein of the innkeeper who did for
Mary and Joseph. Well, the place had been sitting empty for
five months prior. During which time junkies took the railing
off the front steps, what scrap was going for these days. So that
innkeeper business was maybe more than his due.

With Sue gone, cancer last year, he'd have to hire junkie
cleaners for the turnover, didn't have the touch himself with
the broom. Big crack in the top step, moss like velvet lining,
something obscene. Two females, wonder how they got a
porch swing up the stairs. He tried the door and it was locked.
Good sign, sign of consideration for the home. Jessica when

she was little called the giant key ring his jailer's knock. She'd fan it out on the table, that look of concentration that broke in a sly smile. Could he? Couldn't ask Jessica to clean.

He stepped inside. A smell stealthy with mold. He batted the light switch. Nope. Gas? He'd had renters get through a whole winter with no heat, which, they too paid him in cash, the man with the hairdo, pompadour, Quintinar?, the little mamacita, kids tearing around like puppies. He wasn't saying it was Mexicans, but he put utilities in the contract now.

A mattress on the floor in the bedroom, menstrual blood. First time he'd seen the likes of that he'd called the cops, lights and sirens to the crime scene, never thought he'd live it down, as if it was him who'd had a period.

A heap of sheets and a Garfield quilt in the corner. Double-check for sleeping children. It was written in the land-lord insurance. Same as in the school bus insurance, went the agent, all singsong, all the while marking X's where Martin was to sign. Well, no children here. Trash-bag the lot and leave it off at the shelter. What they used to call the pound. Those cement cells open to the weather, it killed him, unearthly howls to their dog-god.

He locked up, stood for a moment gazing across the street into the scrap woods, white pines barely rooted in gravel. That time he—he and Jarnot, come to think, Terry Jarnot—hot-wired his Aunt Mary's Buick, just stupid kids, the whole situation getting away from them.

He wasn't going to reckon with it now, the shit kids do, boys that age. What were they, seventeen? Picked up a girl. Question was, what was she doing walking up on the highway in the middle of the night, anyway? Fair game, said Jarnot.

Honestly didn't occur to them she might refuse. Dumped her out and chased her around in the woods beforehand. Coulda been these woods. Why that came to mind.

*

Casey and Michelle were staying for a time with her dad, Terry Jarnot, house at the head of one of them newer cul-de-sacs, till Casey could get himself employed. Kinda hard when no one frigging hires you, he'd say, like he was having a side conversation with himself, Jarnot looking grim.

First time Casey saw her, Hannah was kicking a stone down the road and he pulled up alongside her. Wanna ride?

She was working on an apple and he had to wait till she finished, her hand in front of her mouth, her eyes like sorry, sorry. What was she, sixteen?

Dark hair filled with stars from the light through the trees in the forest. Big eyes, the brown stirred up from the bottom. The kind of girl who looks away cause her lips are wet from an apple.

I believe we're neighbors, he tried.

He could tell she'd rather kept walking, spring day, you know, but outta consideration and maybe some curiosity she took the ride off him.

The dogs came trotting out when they saw his truck, always so positive, and he watched their tails fall as he drove on by. Boyo followed a few paces but they were yard dogs.

And then a few weeks later, Casey passed her on the road again. Wasn't nothing but a couple minutes in the truck with her till he coasted into her driveway.

You from here, you? He didn't want it to sound like he was flirting. Tried to take it down a level. You from somewhere?

Surprised the hell outta him by pulling her knees up. He was in that frame a mind where he could have kissed her.

He threw his chin at the house and his voice almost cracked, Your mom home?

Again, he didn't want it to be like he was comin on.

She had nothing to add so he strung himself along, Don't mean to pry. Just didn't see you out much before. Myself I'm an open book, could rise to manager if I got the chance, if the job I'm hopin for comes through at Ames—

Then she went and laid her little hand on his forearm. He looked at it like it was something landed there. Whoa. He said, You're gonna make me jump outta my skin you know.

Sittin in her driveway in broad daylight.

Her hand floated to his leg. What the hell? Was he about to get raped? That's what they used to say in high school when a girl was shit-faced, high, asking for it.

What she did then, though.

This one.

Okay.

Put her face right down on his bulge and nuzzled him.

Hey, he said. You know what you're doing?

It came out wrong, but she didn't take it as an insult as she helped him out of his jeans, the whole tight maneuver. She put one hand on his chest to brace herself as she held him at the base and fit her mouth around it. Jesus H. *Fucker*! He looked at the back of her shining head working his lap. He dropped his hands into her loose hair and let himself go. Like that rocket launch down in Florida, the TV screen overwhelmed with red clouds, gray fire—

She sat up and wiped her mouth with the back of her hand.

Fucking hell, he said. Where'd that come from?

He tried—he meant—to look at her respectfully. Mangled his smile. Shoved Michelle right out of his mind. You want me—he faltered, it was too strange. He put his head on the seatback and closed his eyes. Shivered through and through.

Had girls already changed that much since his day? His eyes still closed. He was only twenty-two. He should have opened his eyes and checked on her but part of him was still up there on the moon where the rocket left him off.

He heard himself instead, This your calling card?

I didn't mean that, he started, opening his eyes, and then some crazy little ride, some Dodge fucking Escort came pouring down the street, that pothole dead-end shit, fulla dudes, not one of em he'd like to meet, doing sixty, upwards of sixty-five.

Hannah hit the ground. How he managed to think as fast as he did, but all this time the truck was runnin, cause there's a reason, people were all no war for oil, but if he'd had to locate his keys he never coulda blown outta that trap before them dealers blocked him in. He just floored it.

Terry's poor dogs all confused when he roared by after gettin their hopes up again. He laid down rubber making the turn.

At the highway, the Escort turned opposite.

He breathed, Fucking shit. You okay, girl?

She pulled herself up off the floor.

Say something!

It came out too strong.

He was going too fast. The truck started to shimmy and he relented.

You know them dudes?

Your dogs? said Hannah.

Say what?

I was going to ask you—

Okay, now. Where was she comin from? What was the chance she was touched or something? Had he just been blown by a retard?

She kinda giggled. The names of your dogs.

He slapped the wheel, shook his head. Say *what*?

He gave her a quick look. Well shit. Shook his head again. Well—might as well—we got Boyo, we got Tuna, we got AK, and we got ol Winner.

Looked at her for real now. Fact was he had to pull over at the Shell cause he just wanted to stare.

So, he tried again. You from somewhere?

Not really, she said, doing that thing with her hair.

Okay. Just askin was all. But he felt good, weird.

Just askin, he said again after a while.

What now?

He felt like a shit with Michelle, his smell was off, so he didn't drive down to the end of the street all week. Didn't see Hannah up on the road either. Then Jarnot was asking him to come along and pick up that porch swing.

What?

Ducked out on the rent, said Jarnot, pleased with himself.

Winner the dog needed a boost onto the seat. The other dogs kept their respectful distance.

You ever see them renters much, though? ventured Casey, the noise of his own head filling his ears.

Nope.

So—

Ran into Martin Grenier.

They stomped up to the porch. They were kinda like the repo man. He could tell the old man had misgivings, but Michelle's dad was strong as shit, not that it was heavy, but awkward, you know, stiff limbs. Stood it up in the bed of the Ford like livestock, all forlorn. It was that kind of spring day where the light was a fancy dancer, as his mom used to say.

You and Michelle might take a look at the place, said Jarnot.

Ain't got no work yet.

Jarnot's bill yanked all the way down to his nose. They drove back silent.

The dogs greeted them like heroes, though.

Winner got his bones down and the others sniffed the air, where'd he been, what had he picked up on his travels.

*

It was something to see the fog catch its footing and run against the trees on the other side of the melting field. Year-round squirrels hurried everywhere at once, losing the smell of their corns, worried but not scared enough to change their ways.

Hannah sat on the doorsill of an old outhouse caved into a slope. Last year's brown apples dropped in the princess pine. Her throat stung a little from swallowing.

She could hear Valerie's voice so clearly that Val must be a part of her. Although her foster sister could be high and mighty sometimes. It wasn't a foregone conclusion, sniffed Val. Do you know what that is?

No, said Hannah. Val sighed. She was six years older than Hannah. First of all, she said, softer, but still impatient, you had no obligation to take the ride.

I know, said Hannah, but even Val could see the likelihood that he would have paced her in his truck. There wasn't much shoulder.

Val went quiet. Hannah had been in the empty house almost two weeks. She'd seen Casey playing with the dogs, she liked how he danced, ducking and feinting, psyching them out. She'd seen him with his girlfriend, and he didn't move like that around her. She was so lonely at night she could have walked up the street and got in bed with them.

A motion of protest from her foster sister.

Not literally, Hannah relented, although now she considered it, it seemed more to the point than what she had actually gone and done. A blow job.

The scene rushed up at her again: Casey pulling over at the Shell. You from somewhere? he'd asked.

She'd tried to maintain a small, secretive smile.

You know them sinister dudes? he'd persisted. Then sort of answering himself, I ain't takin you back there.

Thanks, she said, and he'd turned to her with a look of admiration, and it seemed like they could be pals, like maybe next time he was playing with the dogs he'd call out to her as she was passing—

So where am I droppin you off, girl?

She wished he wouldn't call her girl, though.

She gathered her hair and coiled it into a bun with her bare hands, a trick boys never seemed to tire of. Here's good, she'd said, already leaning on the door.

Across the gas station like a melting lake, she hoisted her backpack, crossed the street without waiting for the light to change—and it washed over her that it would've been nice to lie on that bed that was just an ugly old mattress now, her mother had spurted when she hit a vein, and pretend, one more time—

They hadn't even been in the house at the washed-out end of the cul-de-sac half a year when her mother started moving stuff out. Gradually at first, the tube, radio, Paul Revere cooking set with copper bottoms, then all the furniture except the mattress on the floor was gone. Over to her new boyfriend's apartment, she claimed. She promised, when she got it all set up, she'd—

Hannah's clothes too. Hannah didn't see how her mother could have gotten much for a bag of sweaters and jeans.

I am sorry, comrade, her mother had the nerve to say, but I can't take you this time. Got to get out ahead of those dealers— At least she didn't pretend to look Hannah in the eye. Walking out, nothing in hand, she'd tripped anyway, backward into the porch swing. The bench seat caught her at the knees. *When I take you out in the surrey*, she began to sing, on the rebound, pushing with her foot as if it were all choreographed. She could have sung professionally, the swing an aluminum-pitched counterpart. *When I take you out in the surrey with the fringe–on–top!* She patted the seat for Hannah to join her. I have never been to the state of Oklahoma, she said after a while. How many state lines did we cross? And Hannah was forced to replay how her mother had showed up like ten years was a mere ten days, her voice all squeezed, I'm staying clean for you now.

It was the reunion Hannah had imagined so often—so forcefully, it turned out, that she had made it real. She had no one but herself to blame.

She took food from school. The lunch ladies, Miss Helen, a grandma, and Miss Jessica, who once came to the door looking for rent but now pretended not to recognize her, bagged up the extra, and she felt them watching as she slouched away under her big backpack. She got into the habit of saving the waxed green apples, and she lined them up along the kitchen windowsill.

A helicopter growled, shedding late-afternoon shadows, someone's five o'clock news. She told herself she'd done it before, slept rough, on the run, in fact up till she was five years old. Her mother curled head-to-tail and the stars swung low.

She could do it again.

Squirrels shot every which way.

An old tree stand hung off a swamp maple.

An ancient juvenile porcupine stopped to graze off the deer trail.

Mushrooms released smoke. Deer teeth shifted during sex. The setting sun was stretched like rawhide and the porcupine rested on its heels.

Was she near that quarry where kids broke their necks jumping off a ledge three stories high? The other day, a pebble had hit her bare arm and an eerily bland-faced girl, features run out, colors run dry, stepped from the pack and asked was she coming along?

Everyone stared at her as she hesitated. Not your thing? taunted the girl.

There were no-see-ums playing on air.

An old oak leaf propellered and landed softly.

All the news of the forest. Who cared about her news? Growing up was when there was no one watching, and no one to tell. If she found her way back to Pennsylvania, she could live with Valerie though.

The stream had a laugh like heavy furniture. Like someone moving beds, tables, chairs.

Those dealers sure were slow. Her mother already two weeks away. It made her smile.

The wind picked up, and a whole new batch of leaves twisted out over the stream.

NAIAD

She washed up hard. Naked, salted. Uncountable dryout days delivered to the exposed shore, the minutes chiseled in rock and the sun took her for a bone it could bleach with impunity. She bore all the signs of having been wracked by a dauntless lover who after all these years still did not know her human name, nor the shame she had to carry back each and every time—her name was Bethany.

Yeah, yeah. Walk it back, drama queen. Her eyes felt hot off the Xerox. She should have been at work, to state the obvious. Her employee parking spot in the bank's lot had been revoked months ago; now she had to feed the meter, just like the old-sters who stabbed blindly with nickels and dimes, clutching withdrawal slips they'd filled out in shaky script at home.

She crept down the hall to the bathroom and found the tub was full. Old water, no ions. Not a single water lily. Stale, city fluoride smell, and her arm goose-pimpled plunging in to pull the plug from the sexual hole. Down went her soul, glass-eye whirlpool. She was on her knees anyway and she grabbed the side of the tub with both hands to pray. Her sister, a nurse, had once treated her to a day spa, where a sign in the starlit bathroom said, Someday Is Made up of a Thousand Nows.

Same deal, one day at a time.

She felt her daughter and her daughter's friends shake the skinny porch that clung to the house like it was forever trying to get inside. As far as she could tell they were the kind of stoners who thought vodka was for old pervs on park benches and sloppy single moms like her.

Hi Jewel! she called to let her daughter know she was home. The house was the size of a doormat. The kids came laughing inside. Javier wiped his boots like a dog covering up its business, all the while giving her the eye: in a house full of women, he didn't know who had the power, her or Jewel. A couple of girls at work were into tarot, and there were these roles, crone and maiden, virgin and whore.

Hey Ms. Lopresti, said Merk, long-boned, Serbian, with semi-detached ears.

Would you tell your friends it's Bethany? Do you think I like being reminded of my ex-mother-in-law?

Jewel shook her head sadly. Gramma's a honey.

Gramma's the balls, said Javier, heading up the stairs. Bethany heard the bathroom door close. We have mad homework, said Jewel.

For months before her sweet sixteen, Jewel had claimed she wanted nothing for her birthday. Yeah, no, sor-ry, said Jewel. And then without Bethany's knowledge, foreknowledge would be the word, the OG Ms. Lopresti had taken Jewel to get a tattoo. On her still-soft ankle, a roman-numeral-looking

NAIAD. Bethany had been forced to concede, What does it mean?

She could hear them upstairs now, but not the words. She unplugged the microwave and lathered up its nicotine-stained interior. She got in around the private parts of the stove where there was gunk like earwax. At the back of the cupboard she found a mix, let's hear it for Duncan Hines, cool before cutting into squares.

Like all drunks, she was intuitive, fragile as air, and as if she'd called for Jewel, she heard her daughter's mocking voice in the hall again, Someone's been baking, who could it be. The Serbian tree-climber snickered. Bethany waited where she was. She moved along the wall. Stealthy, like a shadow—until Javier jumped, his hand to his heart—Double chocolate? she pleaded.

Aw, Ms. Lopresti.

Sorry, Mom, lied Jewel.

She gathered her coat and her bag and rushed from the house, underlying causes, broken inside. Jewel with her entourage of water sprites, fairies was what they were—No respect, with the exception of her son, Kieran, stationed in Germany, training to be a SEAL. She ground down the street with the emergency brake on. A couple hundred dollars right there. Merko-Croatian and Have-A-Nice-Day were definitely gay. She wasn't prejudiced, but in Jewel's bedroom? Are you all from school? she'd asked, and they'd nodded solemnly. Did you meet in your classes? What's the problem, Jewel? Am I not allowed to have a normal conversation with your friends?

She pulled into the high-school parking lot. Schools were like churches, after school. She would just sit for a while, an island in the middle of a thousand nows. She watched a couple of ladies making solitary laps around the track and her heart went out to them. A half arrow of Canada geese, yakking as they flew by—

Kieran had come out with the ROTC on this very track, and she used to drive over at cocktail hour and watch them drill. Suddenly she needed to be near people, and she felt her mind swarm. Yes, she did, she needed to walk into a bar. She gripped the steering wheel and passed the feeling by. Another way to think about it, said her sister the nurse—recovery, Mary insisted—was rerouting your impulses. Bethany pictured a hatch of demons strutting across the rocks where the minutes were carved, the long nails of their claws leaving exhaust burns. She pictured the route to the roller rink, that birthday party, Jewel in seventh grade—

She burst out of the car and pushed through the low gate onto the track as if she were supposed to start roller-skating. Demon impulses hurled themselves at her empty car.

Her second time around, a little band of detainees was dogged out, likely for some kind of last-ditch, graduation-requirement PE. Chesty girls with shellacked ponytails sailed onto the field. Two big doughboys, coarse hair up in dry buns, pulled out right in front of her, but she found she didn't mind. The all-purpose gym teacher had a hard potbelly that drove his legs apart. How many laps you show us today, Coby? he called. The white kid picked up his waddle speed. How bout you, son? The lightskinned kid produced a minor jog. She used to hate it when other men son-ed Kieran. Don't do this to me, girls! the gym teacher called, and the boys' shoulders sagged. Now Kieran was ripped, with a recon.

The boys were slower than she was and after a few minutes she passed them with a loopy smile. You need men in your life again, Bethany. The wind must have been from behind, because she could hear their conversation now. Imma print out my résumé, bro, take that shit round Home Depot, ten bucks an hour, starting pay.

What was Kieran doing right now, in Germany?

Stack shit all day, you gotta be bettering yourself. The boys walked in silence, and she slowed a little so she wouldn't leave them behind.

My cousin he got a Beamer, six hundred, sell that shit for sixteen, what you do.

One of the boys whistled. Bethany was dying to turn around. See if she could make them smile. Imma get me a Saturday Sunday car, like a toy, bro, you pull up on them bitches be like *yeeeah*.

Shy laughter now. She wanted to laugh with them. The sky was driving the sun down. She couldn't stay out here forever. One by one the other ladies packed it in.

*

Pulling up to the curb at home she felt something tick and she knew she was going to pour a drink the minute she got inside. Okay, she said reasonably. Untick. She waited.

You got this, Bethany. The ticking got louder, propulsive.

If she stayed in the car. If she pulled out again and drove around the block. If she got on the highway and kept her foot on the gas, all the way up to Mary in Medway who had said any time, I will not judge you, Bethany Lopresti, just get yourself to my door—

She bit back tears. Sit tight. The roller rink. A thirteenth birthday party, Jewel all up in the visor mirror every five seconds, kissy lips, wetting down her brows, tightening her hair—You look fine, said Bethany. You too, said Jewel.

Whose birthday?

No one's. She was back up in the mirror. Harper's.

Bethany cackled.

You don't know her. Jewel zoomed in on the little scar above her eyebrow.

Rain had started splintering against the windshield. Everyone was saying it was February in May, the road felt gooey with oil, and the wipers might as well have been nail clippers for how well they were doing the job. Bethany missed the exit and had to improvise, backtracking on the surface streets, leftover houses between six-lane strips of car lots and superstores. They'd already been in the car for an hour.

I don't understand how you always get lost, said Jewel. A bag lady shuffling a shopping cart had started across a broad intersection on green. Bethany stomped the brakes and the car hydroplaned into the turn lane. Slow motion was warp speed. Finally, she felt them bouncing off the curb and she opened her eyes. In the silence that followed, every last one-day-at-a-fucking-time passed.

A heap of crap in the cart, was that an ironing board? A garbage bag of redeemables, a fishing pole. You crazy bitch! shouted Bethany, banging the dash, now flooded with feeling. Did you see that? she turned to Jewel.

The parking lot of the roller rink was nonsensical, unnavigable. It wasn't clear that the featureless metal building had an entrance at all. She gave up and stopped in the middle of nowhere. You don't have to pick me up, said Jewel. How so? And even as she said it, as it stalemated in the air, she saw her daughter watch her begin to dissolve into the just-gifted evening, the imagined pour. It's a sleepover, said Jewel.

She was still sitting in the car. She put her hand on the latch and it was as smooth as glass. If she spent the night right here. If she called Mary, now. She grabbed her bag from the passenger-side floor and felt inside. No phone. One mini. She pulled it out but it was empty, so help me Lord. Just then Jewel and the boys spilled outside, laughing, tumbling into one another down the porch stairs. Jewel saw the car and feigned surprise, paused, waved.

There never would have been a roller rink were it not for the fact that it was Jewel, not Kieran, who was the little smarty after all, and so, seventh grade, Bethany had angled her into private school, even though what was good enough for Bethany was good enough for Jewel. The female head was vain, like only a man should be, and she talked down like a man would, too, like Bethany was Jewel's dumb handler. No one from that school went into the Service, and Kieran felt slighted by his own sister. When he told her he was going to Germany, over the phone, he said, Say bye to Little Miss Harvard for me.

The first time Bethany was invited to a private-school house for dinner she was so nervous she pulled up blotto, and by the time she'd crisscrossed the soft lawn in search of the front door she'd lost a heel. She rang the bell with the other heel in hand, but with the Higher Power on her side, it was the wrong house and no one was home, and she sobered enough in the country air to realize she'd better hustle on out of there.

But soon the finished basements where the kids were flushed the minute they got there all seemed the same. Red or white, Jewel's Mom? Buffet style, plastic plates and utensils—these parties weren't the real parties, she wasn't a fool. She'd end up in the kitchen, clearing her throat as she approached, Anything I can do in here? The hostess would whip around.

Once, one of the many Maddies' moms dropped her voice, You and Jewel seem so close. What's the secret? Those moms could fend her off, but they could lay their traps, too, and for some reason Bethany always gave in. Maybe, she said, because it's just me and her?

Are you single?

My son Kieran—

I didn't know you had an older child!

Yeah. What the heck? Yeah, I do.

It was the Monday morning after the roller rink, and the sleepover, when Bethany got the call. She felt she was justified having her phone on at work because of Kieran, even though at that point he was just out in Texas. Bethany? Everything's fine.

Ms. Lopresti to you? But how had she known it was the head of school? What was she supposed to say? Good to know.

I just wanted to check in toward the end of the year. And to convey how very much we love Jewel around here. The head of school paused. She went around with unwashed, unconsidered hair, and Bethany had not yet been able to work out why this insulted her. I also wanted to reach out because of course I'm a working mom too—Sorry, what?—And with Miss Jewel right here—Come again?

I'm just wondering if she'd shared with you some recent choices she made.

I'm actually at work right now?

I'm aware it's Monday, said the head of school.

Alisha and Pat were staring at her. Alisha sliced her throat, mouthed, Off the phone. Bethany lowered her voice and closed her eyes. Put my daughter on.

Hey Mom, said Jewel.

Are you okay?

Absolutely. No worries.

Great, said Bethany. I'll see you after school. And she dropped the phone straight into the trash.

Jewel came skulking home and toppled carelessly across Bethany's bed on her back in her greasy jeans, making Bethany the imposter in her own room. That stain is nasty, said Jewel. Bethany looked up at the dark yellow shoreline on her ceiling. She'd been watching it for changes every night for years. In case you were wondering what the most disgusting word in the English language is, said Jewel. No.

Soiled. Or the stain looked like a cherub. Bethany crossed her arms. Why did that woman call me today? Stole? Cheated? Lied? Part of her wanted her daughter to show off. To show that private school—I lost my virginity, said Jewel.

A fat cherub blowing a horn. What did you say? But Jewel had closed her eyes. Her face was very pale. And before she could check herself, Bethany heard her own terrible wail, It happened to me in seventh grade, too! The moment the words were out, she knew the mistake she'd made. Never had she betrayed herself like that before. Never imposed her weird, thirsty secrets. Just like that, she was disqualified—as both confessor and protector, and even before Jewel spoke again, Bethany felt the chill off the unknowable, impassable sea that had opened up between them.

After the party, in the parking lot of the roller rink, Harper, Julia, Maddie, and Jewel had all gotten into the car with the high-school boys. I lost my virginity at camp last summer, Maddie had whispered, pressed against the door, in Jewel's ear. I fucking bled like a pig. She rolled her eyes.

And much later, back at Harper's in the silty, early morning hours, the four of them splayed across two queen beds in Harper's bedroom, Jewel, as if she were delivering to them her clearest diamond, creamiest pearl, had spoken up, Well, guess who's not a virgin anymore.

There was shocked silence. Then the silence seemed to shake, and gather momentum as it came crashing toward Jewel. Right before it hit her she looked for Maddie across the room. I was kidding? murmured Maddie.

So, Jewel finished, taking her eyes off the ceiling now, off the water stain, and turning toward Bethany with a mix of disgust and triumph, I don't need you telling me it happened to you too.

FIRST LOVE

The D'Amatas wanted a wake for their little boy at my uncle's restaurant. I'd worked there since my uncle complained he couldn't keep the college girls. At sixteen, I'd thought, my big break. My next big break was getting pregnant with twins. What kind of teen has twins? But the thing was, it made us a family. My mother came around, then my sniffy little sister.

I took some courses and moved into accounts, and flowers. Didn't mind running plates of food when we got slammed on a Saturday, if, I said, I could wear my own clothes. What a flirt, said my uncle approvingly. Oftentimes I knew the ladies who came in, still as tight with each other as they were in high school. Shelby Consiglio, her shop now was Consign with Consiglio, a whole bunch of senior-center acrylic paintings if you ask me, but it was her accompanying Lee Ann D'Amata, asking my uncle if flowers were included, what types of sauce. The little boy was hit by a car, so I knew my twins were safe from a dog's death. It would be stupid not to use a gift like that. I let them draw four-squares right in the middle of River Street, nothing out of me when they shredded the curb, ruining their shoes. Jesus went barefoot. I said, Go ahead, walk a mile to the package store for those silver balloons of potato chips, spend your money on air. Buck your broncos around the superstore parking lot. I said, You two are free since that little D'Amata died for your sins, and they thought I was talking church at them.

The first boy I ever kissed was Joseph D'Amata, the dead boy's dad. Long arms, long, raw neck, sandpaper goosebumps. Three moles made me think of river muck splattered on his right cheek, I never did go skinny dipping. But what gets me now, what kills me, is that he went about his baseball life, chased by girls such as me in the neighborhood, he slid his bony butt under his school desk, just like a lobster tail, all that without sadness. All that with no knowledge of what was to come. Doesn't it seem like the one courtesy Jesus could offer, with those huge grave eyes, would be to spare the innocent? It may sound like church to you, but I am speaking of Joe D'Amata. We kissed like frogs. Our mouths wide and our privates pounding. We wondered if we looked right doing it, if a car passed by and swept us in its headlights, could we be taken for a scene in a movie. Then my mouth and jaw started aching, like chewing gum too long, or having to smile all through a meal with relatives.

My old uncle looked beat to shit coming out of his office behind Shelby and Lee Ann. He paused to cup me. I shook him off. Why did he always have to do that?

THE DISTANCE

"We should have stayed an extra day," said Ray. "Don't you think so, Kevin?" His ears felt like blowholes. Under pressure.

"We could have," Kevin replied mildly.

Ray cleared his throat. He had to project over the highway noise, the static of rain, and he felt like an actor. Ahoy! He felt like a chauffeur. "A whole free day in Boston."

"Mm," said Kevin. He looked up from his phone to gaze pacifically out the window. His baby face made him seem younger than fifty-five, although he must be seventy pounds overweight now. Ray would be sixty in July. Bachelor deacons could count on cake and a card. Ray's parish did a basic chocolate with a very dry crumb. Kevin's served up tiramisu and lemon chiffon.

It was infuriating the way Kevin was hypnotized to that phone. "Well, too late to turn back now," said Ray, considering they were almost an hour south of Providence, with its billboards for God and plumbing services, and the Big Blue Bug, which was just that, something for children to stick in their childhoods. "Do you ever give that thing a rest, Kev?"

Very pleasantly Kevin turned the phone over and folded his hands. "There's just so much to know," he said softly.

True. Once upon a time, Ray had been a very credible English teacher. He would have thoroughly enjoyed seeing the Paul Revere house. He had always appreciated colonial architecture, even though he had to stoop under the doorways. The vernacular quality of the handmade, as if you could hear through the dollhouse panes of glass the tortured conversation of Hester Prynne and the Reverend Dimmesdale. He loved that novel. He respected the drama of the Jesuits, heavy brows and forward thinking, but in his heart he identified with the colonial Protestant, the religious man at large, at home in the town commons and in the world.

"*One if by land—*" he said wistfully, and the highway blew back sheets of sea gray. He was suddenly conscious of wearing the same thin shirt as yesterday. His winter coat, a parka, was stuffed behind his waist, forcing him to crowd the steering wheel. Some sweet old lady had left the parish her canvas-top Cabriolet.

"*Two if by sea,*" echoed Kevin.

Ray's throat tightened. He glanced over but Kevin was distracted again, stroking the glass face of his phone. Ray let the silence deepen.

*

He was still thinking about how much he would have liked to have shown Kevin around Boston's North End. The clattering of hooves, Paul Revere's midnight ride. "Talk to anyone interesting?" said Kevin. It took Ray a moment. "I thought it was kind of austere this year," Kevin added.

Austere? Scripture conference was a petri dish of gossip.

"You remember Joe Nose?" said Kevin.

"From seminary?"

"You've always been a steel trap for names."

"Well, seeing how he used to tie one on."

"Did he ever."

Ray waited. The air was very stale. "He had a funny hat on during the mass," said Kevin.

"Oh yeah?" A truck passing hard spat salt and grit in Ray's eyes against the window. Joe Nose and the brat pack from seminary. Kevin had worshipped those guys.

He couldn't think over the gale force of the defogger. He clicked it down, but the windshield clouded over instantly. Maybe he should be grateful. If he couldn't think, couldn't see— couldn't feel the old jealousy moving in. The fog of jealousy.

The little car wasn't going to crap out on them, was it?

What was so interesting behind that screen? Did Kevin do social media? "Hey," he said, and it came out pleading. "Remember I told you my idea about going as a priest from the roaring twenties?"

Kevin looked up and his screen went dormant.

It was February, Halloween a lifetime away. They'd talked about going to the big party Kevin's parish did together. "Did I tell you I priced them?"

"Did you?" said Kevin agreeably. "Online?"

"Six hundred dollars for the one with a cassock."

"Oh!" said Kevin. "I forgot to tell you I'm going to be in California for my niece Caitlin's wedding that weekend."

Hurt felt like jealously. Jealousy felt more complex than it was.

In the silence that followed, it advanced to certainty that a cough was coming on. The breakfast bar. The breakout rooms. The elevators where they mashed themselves giddily in. He and Kevin had shared a room. Oh, Kevin had said, two queens.

*

Swallowing was painful. Ray tried yawning to relax the hot little throat hole. His feet were cold.

"Can't wait to tell my brother about those guys taking pictures of the building," said Kevin suddenly, brightly. "What was it again?" The Federal Reserve, thought Ray, but Kevin went on, "They were talking in a different language. What do you think it was?"

"Well, they were white," said Ray cautiously.

Kevin leaned forward. "Don't you think there was something? Why would they be taking pictures of the Federal Reserve?"

The ardor of anticipation. Waiting for scripture conference all year could cause the common cold. Or what if it was one of those sinister, snaky viruses out of China, where people blew their noses into their bare hands? Giving in to melodrama, he imagined Kevin venturing into his apartment the morning after he died, calling softly, yet feeling immediately the condensation of the spirit, a cold cloud. It was presumptuous to think that Kevin would run his fingers gently over everything. But he hoped Kevin would be the one to arrange the services. He had named him in his will. And if he didn't die in his sleep, he planned to call Kevin at the final hour. Like the voice of God, Kevin would talk him across the threshold.

Kevin said, "I wish we could see the ocean from here." Out the window an almost devastatingly uninteresting wallpaper of forest. "Do you think we're in Rhode Island?"

Ray said, "You know anybody in Rhode Island?"

Kevin laughed. "Gotta love the calamari, though."

"Cala-mah." Ray's best goombah.

In a funny way, Ray felt like he was listening in. Maybe looking down from above. Kevin beside him in a cardigan, big as a whale. Rain drumming the canvas roof, soon to breach the seams.

*

"What's gonna happen to Harvey Weinstein?" said Kevin.

"Is that on your phone?"

Kevin put up his hands. "I just thought I'd ask."

Traffic slowed suddenly, en masse, and through the spray Ray could make out a semi pulled over, a gnome-like driver with his jacket over his head running around setting up orange cones.

Ray shivered. "Some of those people also used him." He was interested in Weinstein, after all. "To get to a higher position." It interested him how Weinstein did not seem to love women at all. His sore throat was really pulsing now.

"What time do you think we'll be home?"

For a moment, Ray felt bewildered. "You never said if your brother's meeting us in Bay Ridge or Bay Shore." Whatever it was, Ray would drive on to Riverhead. They'd been in separate parishes since seminary. Since Ray left seminary in private disgrace, exiled to teach at Catholic school.

*

Ray's turn to speak passed, and then Kevin's.

Finally Ray said, "Still raining." To state the obvious. "Should we stop for lunch, though?"

"I wish we knew the beaches."

"You always liked winter beaches," said Ray. That feeling afterward, to be warm and dry. Kevin put his palm to the roof of the car just as Ray felt a drop on his bald spot. Immediately he felt even sicker. "You want my coat?" he said anyway, leaning forward. Kevin could pull it out from behind.

"I'm kinda crowded over here."

"Is there anything to do in New Haven?" said Ray.

"There's the Knights of Columbus Museum."

"Is it free?"

"St. Mary's tomb," said Kevin. "The nativity scenes of John Paul II."

"Is that free?" The old banter. Despite himself, Ray's spirits rose.

"They have tours of Yale. Did I tell you my brother's driving for Uber now?"

Ray had been considering a fly on the dash, crisp and lacy like a little Japanese tempura, a very nice passed hors d'oeuvre. Happily, he said, "You have to keep it real clean?"

"I guess you do."

"Does Uber pay you to clean it?"

"I'll have to ask him." Kevin made a humpbacked dive for his backpack on the floor. Bagels. "Did you take those from the hotel?" Ray smiled, holding out his hand. Bread became paste.

So did the body. They ate in companionable silence.

"You see that virus spreading to South Korea?" Kevin said after a while. "I thought about doing my missionary over there."

"I know, Kev." His heart contracted. It was decades ago. And he knew Kevin was more clueless than callous, but still. That kind old sister, Cecilia, she had gone out of her way to counsel him. Had given him the words: *A rejection is not a betrayal, Raymond.*

A rejection wasn't a betrayal. They could still be friends. The Hindus called a line like that a mantra. To be repeated until it became real. Christ's body was the mantra of faith. The persistent pattern of forest out the window was almost antagonizing.

*

Kevin was slaving over his phone again. A car passed on the right and gave them a look like, Assholes. Joe Nose, what a stupid name. Kevin had that fine little Irish nose that must have made the Italian kids want to mash it. Nose wars.

Ray summoned courage, "So, what does it say on your phone?"

"About the virus?"

"Yeah. Sure." Ray waited.

Kevin looked up. His face was flushed. "Social media?" said Ray.

Then, tired of waiting, digging in: "You remember that nun, Sister Cecilia?"

There's an opening in English. Open-minded. *You could jump ship from theology, Raymond.* Meaning, You could avoid bringing your whole life down. And Kevin's. Openhearted. She saved him without judgment. "You remember her, Kevin?"

"She was very understanding." Kevin made an effort not only to look up from his phone but to turn toward Ray. "Very good to you," he added.

And there was the old pain, that hollow feeling, like being winded. Joe Nosotti would have been one to punch Kevin's lights out on the playground and here was Kevin, still in thrall to those regular guys, still refusing Ray's love, his offering. Here was Ray, still in thrall to rejection.

*

"Is that the shirt you wore yesterday?" said Kevin. Ray could feel cold sweat trickle toward the insides of his elbows. He was suddenly self-conscious. His dyed mahogany hair, swollen jowls. "Who was that kid you used to tell me about from there?" said Kevin.

"Where?" Feigning surprise. Buying time—was Kevin toying with him? "Bishop Guertin?" It sounded funny now, the name of that school. Calling Kevin from the same pay phone the boys used. Ray felt himself flush. "Adam Speidel?" It could have been any one of his students.

"I appreciated those phone calls," said Kevin.

Ray cracked his window.

Kevin said, "I always liked your stories."

He needed fresh air, to feel once more sly, indefatigable. He had been a lean and tough young teacher who could give those Catholic boys hell. He put on a voice, "If you're not sitting right in front of me I'll crucify you, Adam. Why are you a major wise guy?" He laughed at himself. "That's what their parents wanted, reform school."

"And you, a seminarian," said Kevin.

Was that admiration? He'd written letters, too. Learned to take comfort in pouring his heart out to Kevin, always in his head and sometimes on the page. Exiled by Sister C.; rebuffed or not, he carried Kevin with him everywhere. Rejected but not betrayed. Kevin had never written him back, not a single word.

"Hey," said Kevin, tearing the last bagel in half. "Isn't this New Haven?"

"I think it's New London," said Ray, before he could register dismay. There was that pastoral view of the riverbank, a far shore that he always thought of as holy land. Had Kevin already moved on? And then, a mounting resurgence of the old need to exert force, force Kevin to pay attention to him— "Didn't you have a cousin who lived around here?"

"I do," said Kevin.

"Did you stay over that time?"

"When?"

"With your cousin?"

"I'm not sure."

"Is he married?"

Kevin would have been the kind of priest housewives creamed for. "Did he come to the wake for your father?" Ray was thrashing. "Would I have met him there?" As if jealousy could close the distance.

*

They drove on in gaping silence. How long could it last? He knew his attention was oppressive. Kevin had once told him it was the way his mother had loved him. He had admitted to Ray that from time to time he regarded other men as objects of desire. For example, Joe Nose. He had gone so far as to ask Ray who he thought was the best-looking seminarian. He used distraction like a shield. It wasn't fair. And the way he was not insecure but indecisive—it drove Ray crazy.

"I was thinking," said Ray finally. He took his time. It was something he'd been turning over lately. "No one ever called us athletes."

"What do you mean," Kevin said uncertainly. "In school?"

"It would have changed our lives."

"Think so?" said Kevin.

"They say school of hard knocks but I don't know. School of negativity. What if they were like, Kevin!" All the way across the field. "Cleanup hitter!" Oh, it felt good to shout it. "Superstar!"

"Ha." Kevin couldn't help but grin. "You think I wouldn't have gone to seminary?"

Ray said impatiently, "You know guys at seminary played ball."

But Kevin spoke almost wonderingly now. "Choose up teams. Called him coach and it was just gym class. It was hu-miliating. I'd always be one of the last five."

"I'd be last," said Ray.

Kevin closed his eyes. "Mother Teresa always said, God doesn't measure our success, He measures our faithfulness." Kevin paused. "I did feel very small."

Don't break my heart now. But Ray's heart if not broken had broken off, and it moved in his blood so that the ache was even in his feet and hands. He was unsure for a moment if the car was still moving. He felt the foreshadows of trucks on both sides before they dwarfed the Cabriolet simultaneously.

*

But he couldn't help himself. "Did you stay overnight for that funeral in Cos Cob?"

"What?"

"Kevin," said Ray. For just a moment, he felt in control. *Monsignor.* Kevin was silent.

He had to give up this line of inquiry. Interrogation. He vowed to quit stalking Kevin's whereabouts. God gazed upon them, rendering distance useless. He felt for his own phone and found it in the grotto of the gear shift.

"Did I show you a picture of our dog?" He was pleading— to start over. "She looks like a little fox, doesn't she? That's our parish dog now."

"A little fox for sure." Kevin cradled Ray's phone in both hands. "She a rescue?" Ray nodded. "So you think it was as good as last year?" said Kevin.

"I liked it better in Philly." Ray paused. "Did Joe Nose come to Philly?"

"And Joe Vincello, and Frank Colomaria, and probably Frank Macintyre was there," said Kevin.

"I used to have nightmares about that nose."

"Yeah, the nostrils." Kevin snorted accidentally, giggled. "Hey." As if the sky had cleared, "I recognize that bridge."

"Yeah," said Ray. "New Haven."

INHERITANCE

It was the day of her party. Serena curled onto her side like a girl. She remembered opening her eyes in the middle of the night to see the moon wavering—and a single persistent star, separated from its flock as if on purpose.

She patted for a tissue and bumped into a book on her bedside table. That stingy, high school–issued Flannery O'Connor she'd brought upstairs when she was picking up for the party. The glue was as dark as molasses and chipped like enamel so that the little volume was more a stack of tarot cards than a paperback. The pages were the color of brown eggs, as if they'd freckle off on her. First thing you used to do, she thought, was hunt down the autograph of the previous Highland student to whom you were now indelibly lineaged, a name that might taint you or promote you, or merely bring you closer to graduation.

The cover was carved in ballpoint where it had served as a hard surface for composing love notes. She could have taken a rubbing. That dread thing, Miss Scully, old maid of eleventh-grade English, balding, gray teeth seemingly strung, apt to clatter, turned and wrote the letters AGMIHTF on the blackboard. Like the days of the week on the plastic pillbox-es that went skating across Serena's grandmother's kitchen counter. Grammalah had calculated, and come up from the South when Serena started high school. "My window of influence," she declared, and she made sure to pronounce *Connecticut* with all its letters, as if she were distinguishing the Algonquian. Serena's family money was her money, although it would be years till she relinquished it. She held fast to her mannered drawl as well, and her outré wickedness. Everybody knew she was foundationally committed to her prejudices, but as Serena's mother said primly, you could still love her.

Serena could hear her own daughter, Bella's rebuttal, Could you? If Serena could summon her wits after one of Bella's ambushes, she would accuse her daughter of loving on condition.

Miss Scully's students were to put down on a clean sheet of binder paper what they thought the word "good" meant in the title of the story collection.

"A Good Man Is Hard to Find."

Boys drummed their desks, girls tittered, except for those feminists who were practically writing in blood. Without a moment's hesitation Serena wrote on her loose-leaf: "Good for marriage."

Now she slid the relic into the drawer, where yesterday she'd stowed her grandmother's embroidered antimacassars. The skill and fancy in the intricate border of bluebells and violets, all the things that girls used to do, apparently. She'd redrape them on the arms and necks of chairs and sofas after the party; they were prone to peel, hitch rides on people's sleeves and collars. William's death a decade ago had made her a young, old-fashioned widow. Grammalah too, widowed before forty. Suddenly the morning sun, fresh out of a can, poured into her bedroom—

And the day landed, packed solid with duties. Serena had agreed months ago to host the benefit, aimed at a circuit of small-time multimillionaires, prematurely paunchy scions and heiresses who relished being pried like oysters, all of whom must be seduced, and pledged early, before they slipped out, selfish with alcohol and dinnered up with morsels.

She looked with dismay at the orphaned outfits cast about her bedroom as if she were a teenager. Her face was smooth although she was almost fifty. The moon would have to be her sun, Grammalah had instructed, fingering Serena's cheeks like Sea Island cotton, and indeed she had retained something of a moon-wax complexion, a maiden-like composure, and on more than one occasion she and Bella had been mistaken for sisters. The sun was a decoy in her full-length mirror.

Bella took after William, a daughter as strong as a son, her handsome square jaw and dark, brushstroke eyebrows. Moral yet carnal, formidably self-justified.

She looked askance at the earth-toned Indian blouse with the tassels, the sailor dress that had seemed so fun when she and Bella bought them together. Did Bella wear hers? Serena wouldn't dare ask her. She was flagging already. Oh yes, she'd been coerced into giving this party, strong-armed by a cadre of extroverts—her closest friends. Jen Perloff and Gayathri Sheridan and Annie Ackerman. "But I really might hate people," Serena had said feebly.

"You're just shy," Jen dismissed her.

Case in point, she hated sweating on her raft in a close flotilla of other rubber rafts at yoga. She was privately appalled that the teacher wore a microphone. In all honesty, she could peck around the health-food store two or three times a week, chat with the cashier-owner, and her social needs would be satisfied.

Her friends had slipped into a teasing charade of trying to match her up with someone. It was, Serena supposed, their way of venting the airlessness of her mourning. They felt stupid, useless, asking her the same questions year after year: Are you okay? Do you miss him? They still organized moms' nights out for her. She couldn't tell them she missed the company—the male energy—of their husbands.

Gayathri texted, "*bux?" and Serena sent her a smiley face even though she had quietly quit drinking coffee. She pictured Gayathri all bust in a camel turtleneck sweater, requesting a cardboard carrier for two lattes, balancing out to her car, using her big hips for ballast. They'd met years and years ago at fencing. Gayathri's son was one of those homeschooled kids with an outstanding name, explained Bella. Now Maple was at Yale, and Bella at Bowdoin, but Serena could still see her daughter en garde, back leg loaded, fierce and faceless in her mask, rush and retreat, clashing foils, sabers, épées like cymbals, fighting her grief at the death of her father.

Gayathri punched her horn outside and passed the latte through the window. "You sure I can't do anything?" She was enthroned in the cognac seats of her vehicle.

Serena tucked her hair behind her ears. "No, no. This is so sweet of you."

Gayathri tipped her sunglasses back down and shrugged herself deeper into her leather. "Well, I'll be there in all my splendor."

She gunned off and Serena watched the taillights. She was a goddess. Along with a pantheon of tutors, Gayathri had homeschooled Maple from first grade through high school, dressed every day as if she were going to work—edging out Anna Wintour. Serena was in jeans and a plaid shirt for now, moccasins. Did Gayathri know it was a little bit disingenuous for her to give this party? Gayathri's husband was an incredibly hardworking consultant. Serena could so easily have contributed twice as much as whatever would be raised for tonight's charity. She could have quadrupled it. In a way, it was false of her to live here among regular mortals. Naturally they assumed she was one of them.

Speaking of mortals, six hours till she opened her home to nosy hounds and slinky cats, with some mice scampering in too, for the cheeses. She would take the first drink orders herself, modeling for the two college girls she'd hired to circulate, giving the illusion that the event was a natural extension of her shyly flirtatious spirit. Voices would fill in as the animals multiplied with their farm and forest babel, striving to understand one another; or not animals exactly, but Serena knew she would feel like Dorothy in *The Wizard of Oz*, a large human girl among creatures.

The caterer had come and gone twice already, and trays of finger food took up every surface of Serena's kitchen. The landscapers had shaved the garden into submission; the Vine Shoppe folks had come by in their Eurovan with the cases; one of the quirky local breweries had dropped off the kegs she had ordered to surprise and please her friends' husbands. Her housekeeper had popped her head in, and Serena herself had arranged tulips in Georgian vases and positioned them all around her house. It was an old trick of Grammalah's, to let people know you knew they were snooping. There was a bouquet on a dresser in her bedroom.

She was still standing with the coffee on the sidewalk, the sun making arabesques around her. She should've just texted Gayathri for a decaf; she hated, now, to toss the alpaca-colored elixir, but in a self-conscious jerk of disgust she splashed it against her bushes. She went through the side gate with its crescent-moon cutout—William's idea, for little Bella—and into the garden.

She owned a sculpture by an "associate," the dealer had said, of Calder; a stabile, as opposed to a mobile. She half dreaded and half thrilled to the day Bella might ask her why she hadn't just bought a Calder. Would she say it was because no one in this town would have known the difference? Her stabile, in any case, was the same powder-coated Chinese red, and built around the same tilted axis of flight as a Calder. There was something extraterrestrial about it, both light and lumbering. William had had it bolted into its own concrete square and insured separately. Oh William, the thief who had stolen her out of art school, Grammalah would say. "It makes you less virginal not to have finished, Sally." She loved her little brushes with the vulgar.

Serena's trust fund matured at her marriage. It was her mother who had stammered it, if not quite on Serena's wedding night then close to it, as if she were confessing to a Victorian daughter that marriage could lead to children. And Grammalah was right, it had seemed suddenly pointless to stay in college. Wealth assumed you knew who you were already.

She put her hand on the sculpture. She and Bella had spent a long weekend in Washington, D.C., last year, visiting the museums on the mall, treating themselves to a hushed hotel and, according to Bella, happening restaurants. In the National Gallery, they had hovered over a series of Ellsworth Kellys and Serena had felt almost disembodied. The sentient shapes of color were no less than the building blocks of the world. "He really is my favorite," she'd said softly. That's what she would have painted, she thought, had she stayed in school. Pursued a career. Depictions of the thin plane between inner and outer worlds. She would have painted herself serene, like her name, both detached and profound. To be exempt, yet full of feeling. "I should have been a gay man," she whispered.

Bella bucked in surprise, but without missing a beat she whispered back, "If you mean a gay *white* man."

Serena ignored the correction. She didn't care what color. She remembered when Grammalah had finally learned she was supposed to say "people of color." "And what am I, Sally? A person of pallor?"

Serena could hardly boast to Bella that she had once tried to save Grammalah from embarrassing herself.

In the Calder room she was struck by how much more pleasing it was to watch the shadows of the swaying mobiles than the mobiles themselves. Swaying wasn't the right word. In Serena's peripheral vision a middle-aged woman with un-colored hair stood rocking as if she were still soothing an infant. Serena looked at Bella across the gallery, her neck jutted forward unbecomingly, gripped almost obtusely by her phone, lost to her surroundings. It hurt her when her daughter dropped her guard, forgot to be lovely.

Serena drifted over. Bella had paused inadvertently before a photograph of Calder's momentous "Eagle." It lived at a sculpture park in Seattle, apparently. Bella sensed her presence and looked up, producing a goofy smile. Heading off reprimand, she wrapped her arms around Serena and said duskily, "I love looking at art with you, Mommy." She rested her head for a moment on Serena's shoulder. "I can never figure out how long to stare at something and I just let you guide me."

Oh, Bella. She wanted to say something encouraging. "You used to be such a creative builder, Bell." Then all in a rush, "Honestly, these amazing symmetries, wooden blocks and Legos, but also—" she hadn't remembered until she said it, "a porcupine made out of dry spaghetti!" She laughed. She knew her eyes were alight with need, "Cereal boxes cut up and chinked into a log cabin!"

Then a shockingly gaunt young man in running tights and a Vanderbilt Law sweatshirt came into the gallery and they both turned. He was African American. Earbud lines dangled from his hand like Calder wires. When he was out of earshot Bella said, too evenly, "You looked at him a certain way, Mom."

Moments passed. "I think I'm ready for lunch," said Serena finally, which had the desired effect, and her daughter followed her almost meekly from the museum.

In the end, Serena had to admit she found Washington a common circus. The crowds depressed her, groups speaking in sign language, high-school marching bands, chaperone dads in cargo shorts, nasty-looking babies, blithely unselfconscious liberal-arts girls sucking those outdoorsy water bottles. She didn't want Bella to see the city through her tired eyes and she was glad when they escaped, the taxi swinging around the Potomac to the airport.

It had turned into a chilled glass of an evening. The women would bring wraps, or, later, Serena would offer her own sweaters. She had managed to break a nail where it bled and she worried briefly that the Band-Aid made her look like an old lady. The bartender, overweight, in a cheap uniform, was setting up on the patio behind a folding table.

The college girls came in Black and white. Saying it that way would surely offend Bella. The white one had an ingratiating laugh and servile posture; the Black one went ahead and listened to music from her phone as she polished glasses, precluding conversation. Serena had to admit that every single Black person made her feel self-conscious, like a nondancer.

Then the doorbell rang, and she heard herself saying, "Here we go!" as she set herself in motion, lightly across the porch, through the kitchen where the caterer was helicoptering over thimble crab cakes.

Napoleonic little Jen, and Alex—the Perloffs. Serena held her breath, deerlike, for half a second then kissed them in turn and Jen was already piping her head around, mouthing, "Gorgeous." She walked the Perloffs through the house and out the back and already the garden was shivering. Her borders recently redone with pea gravel, it was in all the magazines, a row of olive trees in old terra cotta, jumbo white tulips, but now she feared the garden looked bloodless. The doorbell rang again, and Serena skipped away, her heart pounding.

Soon enough the party was underway. Both the college girls, thank God, seemed to have got the hang of it. The little pizza bites she had thought would be too garlicky seemed nourishing in the colder weather; and it was poignant how Jen and Gayathri and Annie were acting like satellite hostesses, working their tails off for her. People were admiring the almost-Calder, other people were grouped around the garden statuary girl, bare breasted in her cement brocade, cupping her hands like Saint Francis.

Serena hurried here and there, she was a point of light, baiting this or that conversation. Were people starving, cold, in need of a napkin? Did they like the "free-range" beer? She thought to call it that on the spot. To her aural left, somebody's daughter wanted to drop out of college—Serena turned and it was Tina Mandel in female CEO attire, Tina's daughter and Bella had done T-ball together. Or was it tennis? "Have you tried service learning?" offered a board member Serena had not yet been introduced to. "Ecuador?"

Ecuador—Bella had been on such a program. Had wandered sun-splotched streets with raw sewage in the gutters, fended off angry young men, wandering farm animals.

"She did a semester in the DR," said Tina, "but it really wasn't very meaningful."

The Black college girl appeared at her side, offering the tray, and Serena pursed her lips and shook her head tightly. Did the girl not recognize her? Her mood had shifted. Jen caught up with her and snuggled close. "Guess who texted me." Some divorced father Jen was trying to set her up with.

"I'm too nervous." When had she signaled that she was readily available? Jen rolled her eyes. Serena felt herself pulled backward and sideways, an impossible diagonal which made her think of her blind spot in tennis.

It was Tina Mandel, closing up to volley—"*Tell* me who did the floral," and Serena knew people assumed she had a decorator, she hated to disappoint them—

"You're all up in those design magazines, aren't you," Bella had said recently. Was Serena imagining a sexual insinuation? Luckily, here was Annie, and Serena latched onto her friend, who appeared to be wearing one of Bella's faded old hoodies over her little black number. Oh, how Serena warmed to the picture of Annie slipping upstairs to Bella's room, guessing where to find things. She would climb in Bella's skin too, if she could. She looked around her party, all the pink faces.

In an argument they'd had recently on the phone, Bella had accused her of pathologizing her, Bella's, interest in social justice. "I'm all for reparations, Bell, really," Serena had tried. No secret that she only ever wanted to return to her daughter's good graces. "And I would pay your share. I just honestly don't like them telling me they judged me and found me—"

"Ah," said Bella. "But we're all racist."

"I don't like their anger," Serena forged onward, "I think of, you know, a Gandhi."

"Jesus!"

Serena laughed, "Him too."

For a moment, Serena thought it was going to blow over. But then she heard Bella take one of her power breaths, and gathering her forces, the force of nature that was her daughter began, "Let's say your third owner, Mom, mortgaged his house on you and defaulted, and sold me off across two state lines. Without you."

"What are you talking about!" Serena interrupted. "It's not our history." There was silence.

The silence began to reel. But Bella had never really heard her side of the story. "Did I ever tell you about Grammalah's maid?" said Serena.

Bella let out a choked cry. "Emma?" Serena persisted. But a terrible knowing was opening inside her. How could Emma the maid have been, as Grammalah claimed, her best friend? Serena wouldn't repeat it. Her eyes longed to close, but she forced them open. "Bell?" she said. "We're all born innocent."

"No!" cried Bella.

You were. How had she had raised such a fearsome girl, rigid, righteous, estranged from her own precious childhood? Bella had begged to go to a boarding school with a mandate for diversity. There was no life worth living but one that changed the world. How bitter her disappointment when she realized that the students of color weren't as struck by fellow feeling as she was.

Yet in the end, by sheer persistence, force of will, Bella had prevailed on a young history teacher, a Haitian American named Esther Henriques. "My mentor," Bella introduced her solemnly at graduation. She was a very slight and ruby-dark person—Serena knew she wasn't supposed to notice the Pantone of her skin—with swinging gold discs at her ears that caught the sun and threw it past Serena.

"Miss Serena," she said, with a laugh in her voice and an enormous, winning smile.

She said to Annie now, "Will you hold down the fort while I go pee?" and Annie waved her away. It was Bella who had taught her to say "pee" instead of "ladies'."

She passed the powder room and went all the way upstairs. Quiet. What if she never returned? Her bathroom was jumbled with expensive flights of creams and capsules. She checked the mirror. She had terribly thin hair and it had blown the wrong way. Bella's hair was a rich, dense chestnut—daughters were always getting their father's manes. William used to cup Bella's baby skull. Rare as lightning, or so they say, to die in a plane crash. Just a toy, a Cessna Skyhawk, the client doubled as a ruddy, glad-handing pilot with a very tall third wife William had happily described as "one of the boys." She would have perched gamely on the case of champagne. Serena had always trusted that he wouldn't have been afraid in the moment, as the flimsy thing went down. That he would have been absolutely sure of his survival.

The bathroom window looked down on the garden and Serena pulled the blind aside. She could see the evening birds tinkering with the budded branches. But look how her garden was sunk in shadow, as if the party were already over. Grammalah cut in, goading her as always, "Awfully shy for a debutante, Sally." It would be dark before she made her remarks, at this rate. She closed the lid of the toilet and straightened the hand towels. She had made notes: how she met the director of the nonprofit years ago, how she was continually wowed by the transformations effected, the turnarounds, the absence of federal dollars, the operating deficit, the dependence of the organization on generous donors—"You knew it was coming!" she would insert disarmingly. Now she arpeggiated down the stairs, through the kitchen and outside, where old men in acute navy jackets were rocking like lobster buoys.

There was gentle applause following her speech, and then the director of Raring to Read, the beneficiary—no, she corrected herself, it was the low-income minority children who would benefit—took the helm.

She slipped inside again. She was freezing. Her kitchen was inhabited by the caterer, whose eyebrows had recently been singed off. According to Jen she was vastly overqualified, and sober, and behold, her canelés might as well have been winged.

Serena herself felt lightheaded. Back out on the porch, out of the light, she missed William with a force that nearly knocked her backward. She opened her eyes and wrapped both arms around a pillar. William had been as firm and tall and strong when he died.

Of course, she couldn't sleep afterward. She had a simple theory about sleep, that it was the single predictor of success in the world. The party ate her alive as she lay awake in darkness. She always felt as if she'd misbehaved, no matter if she had a sip of wine or five glasses. She must have offended or been incomparably dull; she was certain people went home disappointed. She saw all those open faces, pinks and reds and purples. Furry ears, rows of chompers, gray roots, blackheads, face powder. Tomorrow her inbox would be stretched long like a Christmas stocking: thank you, lovely, what a dream.

She reached across the empty bed, felt for the drawer and poked her hand inside. There was the little book, cool to the touch. She brought it to her chest before she turned the light on. Good for marriage. Girlhood to widowhood. Anything with a hood sounded old. Serena recalled that Flannery O'Connor was a spinster who lived with her mother. Bella had always been speeding away from her.

To eddy in place—that was the motion she'd been trying to describe, her native rhythm—like a Calder mobile.

She thought about getting up and putting all her clothes away. Was it that kind of sleeplessness? Bella had a particular way of roaming the house, restless but also reclaiming, as if she were spreading her scent, or reorienting gravity.

She had picked up the book last time she was home. "You've always had this book around," she said affectionately.

"Borrow it!"

Tentatively Bella turned it over. "Was it one of Dad's?"

Later Serena was at her desk in the alcove off the kitchen when Bella rushed in, wielding the paperback. "God, Mom! This thing is *racist*!" She stood there blazing. "It just proves everything in my Race History seminar, it's unbelievable!" She looked more beautiful than ever. Aroused, was the word that came to Serena's mind. Did she think she'd smashed Serena's idol?

She narrowed her eyes. "Was it Grammalah's?" She was offering a way out, and Serena wavered.

She had marked a page and now she opened the book and as if to read aloud. "Do you not see the way Flannery O'Connor uses Black people? As the freak show that startles the real characters, the white people, to revelation?" She was flushed once more. "As the hoop they have to jump through to get to all that redemption and mercy?"

Briefly Serena was surprised that such a thing was incriminating. Her daughter made a denigrating hiss that she had learned out in the world.

"I thought it was a love story," said Serena.

Bella's mouth was still open. Her eyes were wide, trying to comprehend her mother. "Have you read it?"

Serena shrugged. Her turn to shock her daughter.

She got out of bed and she felt as if she were dragging the bed behind her. Down the stairs, out the back door onto the porch—the garden was molded into a square of darkness, the air dank like water. She stood as if at the edge of a dock, looking for light, or the depths of shadows. Soon she could see the tall shapes of her very own stabile, and her cement-cast mannequin, as if she had raised them herself. Bella used to dress the statuary like a snowman in scarves and mittens, and William would stride loose-limbed, laughing and scheming, across the garden to join her.

How was it that her father's death had made Bella a more serious—a better—person, but had only depleted Serena?

Oh, how she missed him. There were so many different kinds of missing—loss was a shapeshifter, constantly renewing and reinventing itself. She believed for second that she could raise William from the garden too, just as sculpture and trees had taken form from the dark—

And then indeed she did see something, not a ghost, but a decision revealed, and she knew what she must do. It came as fast; it came as if it were conjured.

She would cut Bella loose.

Let her go.

All at once Serena's mind was set in perfect motion. To-morrow she would make an appointment with her lawyer, she must call first thing—she would free her daughter from the weight of implication Bella felt to be so terrible, free her daughter from her inheritance.

That was the love story Serena would write, if she were Flannery O'Connor.

STOP IN FOR A FREE COFFEE
IF YOU'RE FROM ARKANSAS

The apartment turned out to be a crash pad on concrete behind a garbage-filled courtyard. Her sons rode their bikes right in, like men living with horses. The trunk of the toilet was cracked, and cockroaches pimped the rim. The shower curtain was a towel she didn't recognize, meaning it didn't come from home; on closer inspection, loose contrails were bloodstains. But she was a nurse, nothing scared her except airplanes, a fear like a vaccine against fear, and she'd made Cal and Edward promise not to fly. Never mind. From the beginning, they'd been fused to two wheels. They'd figured out how to fix them, how to steal them back from teenagers, and by seventh grade, they were male domestics, butlers to their drug dealer, careful with their dreams.

Dad, their dad, was a lineman. He'd been working Saturdays for the overtime, and when she woke up late that morning, his side of the bed, as they say, was already cold. When he died that's how it would be. She made her way to the kitchen but he'd been gone so long the coffee he'd left in the pot was sheened over like gasoline. She looked out the window. He'd put up the snowman flag for her years ago and once again its season had come around. Today was Cal's twenty-fifth birthday.

Twelve blocks to the station, where she stood gasping in the shallows until the conductor brayed, "Stand by for the ten fifteen!" She changed in Newark for the PATH train.

One cigarette, a beacon, a torch, to navigate crosstown. At least she knew how she would die. She steered into a bodega for flowers, pushing the plastic tent aside, who was she to say if the flowers were real despite the fact that they had no scent and came in colors like nail polish. A girl in a Santa hat reeled past. A businessman stopped midstream to say, "My wife?" Did he think the sidewalk was the privacy of his own home? The phone seemed tiny, negligible, the way he pinned it with one huge finger to his ear. "Not at all." A booming laugh. "She's a tall blond, looks like she's a lot of fun." As if he pressed a button, the exact same laugh—"But don't they all, at that age."

They'd tried marriage counseling after Cal overdosed the first time. But she couldn't bear to see Dad disoriented, unmanned. Saturday mornings he'd conducted cursory room checks, taken them to the barber, the hardware, the fire station. Now all his common sense was undermined by a new code. She passed a bald park with baggy squirrel nests scaled in camo sycamore trees. The sun was rotting like a lemon. She missed her boys, their fleet of bicycles tangled in the garage, they wove in and out of the house all weekend for years.

There was a shiny squeeze pillow of ketchup on the sidewalk. Another boy would step on it and squeal.

The windows of a coffee shop were festooned with colored lights and a lighthearted sign on the sidewalk was meant to entice her in. Not literally her. What was the age at which young people began to own the world? Their age or hers?

Just as she began to fear the avenue was coming to an end, the numbers matched, the grated door was ajar, and there was a set of half stairs and a narrow passage that came out into a courtyard. She looked up to see that the tenement rose six floors but was blocked on all sides by other tenements. She missed her step and tripped forward, catching an old metal trash can. Dad could always be counted on to watch cartoons with them when it rained. The can clattered and rolled, leaving a wet trail. A muscular seagull resettled, slit its steely eyes.

She found the buzzer. Not so different from knocking on their door when they were outgrowing their twins, sticky feet hanging off the frames. Those years the purpose was to sort the naturals from the unnaturals. Twelve-, thirteen-year-old boys, sweet and sour with fresh testosterone, under the impression they were baseball stars. Not her boys.

But then there was Edward at the door, trying to make sense out of a petitioner with a sleeve of flowers, the lost wife of some old man. When she saw in his eyes that he remembered his own name, she said, "It's Cal's birthday." He let her follow him inside. Cal was passed out along a sofa, boots and all. He looked made of wax, but she was sure his hair breathed. She laid the funny flowers on his chest. The place was dark, yes, but it seemed to have a different gravity. A force she couldn't resolve.

SOLDIER

The first few years of your twenties
everything in your head is in the second

person. You like

how it sounds

both universal & intimate.

You don't know yet that youth is an anomaly—
although your innocence is getting cryptic.
Your suffering is high calorie, your love sweats like a glass of water—

You travel to France, where your
homesickness is claustrophobic.

Your best friend is in Senegal, and you talk about meeting
in Morocco. You drop
pocket-
fuls of coins
in a pay
phone

at a cross-
roads in a village clad
in cobble-
stone.

In Amsterdam you're Van Gogh,
in Budapest a vegetarian, back
in New York, you're a parade of roommates.

You live on cash, you wear boots in summer.
You grab rides off taxis on your rollerblades, and
only once does a cabbie try to scrape you off against a parking meter.

Another cabbie shows you his match-
maker's album on a long ride you can't afford. He waves you out into the night
with his blessing.

Nights
days
packs
of wild dogs under the L
in Bushwick
where you live
with no telephone
& a scavenged
vacuum cleaner.

You're on your
own. Those
are your own

words. All the fast
new words make
language smaller on purpose.
You don't have the heart to do that to language, to make
it sound stupid. You devour your staff
meals, you wash your underwear
by hand, you save
your cash in your dirty
laundry—the dirty
corners of your consciousness curl

to make an envelope.
Inside, you find
you're going to Russia.
As much of a surprise to you as
to anyone.

Late afternoon, the winter sun strung along a last gleaming wire, you look up
airlines at the post office.
Deep-discount roundtrip
to Moscow on Air India,
but you're told that if you want to pay cash
you must purchase the ticket in person at the airport.

You borrow a car. You find
your friend's car blocks
away from where she said it would be, and
as you approach, you see it's sunk
low on one
back tire.

Oh, no.
You know
what that means.
Your friend's car is just this ancient nasty Subaru
held together with bungee cords & duct tape, and you're tempted

to sneak away. You see yourself heel-toeing
backward.
The curbside back
tire sitting on its rim
on the pavement.

You dig around in the glove compartment for the manual, and you assemble
the tools & the jack
& the spare on the sidewalk.
But when it finally comes to it, you aren't strong enough to turn
the lug nuts.

You find the AAA card in the glove compartment
and you stow
the jack
& the playtools
& the spare
and you walk back
to the pay phone
at the post office.

When the AAA operator answers, you burst into tears in your own country.

Hold on, hold on, what borough?
You're sorry—
and you cry
that kind of female song-
crying, because with a clarity
you won't have again
for decades, you understand
it's no country for women.

The mechanic is an old guy with hands
twice as big as the biggest penis you've ever seen,
in pornography. You think he's wearing gloves,
but then you realize that stuff
is his skin. No thumbnails.

You guess you
have a slow leak, you
say. You say you
think the rims
are all bent up—you

notice he's noticeably
silent. A slow leak?
you repeat yourself.

You're feeling around in the dark for his rhythms.
You want to be understood.
At the same time, you're pretending
to be your friend, it's your friend's AAA card, so it's like you're standing by
in black jeans

& a little leather
jacket.

                                    Pretending to be
                                        your friend,

you say the tire holds for a week—
you recall as you're speaking that this is what your friend told you—
and then you wake up one morning,
and it's down on you.

                    The second person is getting crowded.

Uh-oh, says the mechanic. His right eye
kicks out sideways, level with the ground.
You gotta watch out for that, he says, his eye
in the gutter. He pauses.
Your attention is ardent.
Don't go falling asleep, he says. No way.
He pauses.
He'll be down on you in a second.

You feel a small shock
as the clammy humor registers. Then you imagine the juices
stinging the back of the mechanic's throat
and you look at him again with sudden reverence.

                                    That very spring,
                        you find yourself in a Tolstoyan village.

Suddenly language thinks before it speaks.

There's lightning in the morning
that dries out the clouds as Galya weeds
the bed of red zinnias under your window.

What do you do all day in America? says Galya.

Now that the butter
is made in loaves,
and the bread rises
in the hospital for bread,

you laugh nervously. You whicker,
you're only twenty-two.
When Galya was twenty-two—she squeezes
her eyes at you. Life
is more serious in Russia.

She looks at you intensely and you hang your head,
just to get it over with.

You notice that for a moment
the two of you breathe together.

You fall in love accidentally,
and your heart hurts like a stomach.
He lights a short snag
of tobacco,
surveys the clay dirt

from behind his mullah beard,
his work pants cinched around his waist as skinny
as a finger.

There's a skeleton of lightning.

This storm has horns, he says,
putting his fingers on his head.

The sun flickers and goes out.

He climbs up to the very top of the tractor.

The zinnias against the stone sky, the tractor
shaking, the engine thunder—

He gives you a little wave

and you throw yourself down on the dirt.

You may be passive,
pawn-like, in the second
person, but you
get up before he runs you over.

His wife, Galya, calls at your window,
Come on, get your swimsuit!
You watch her march
toward the pump, empty
buckets, workhorse

shoulders.
Her field-grass
hair braided
down her back,
big, dimpled
legs, she's more
than beautiful enough
to be enormous. It bowls
you over. Everything overflowing
her Soviet bikini.
Fifteen years
older than you, fifteen
times more beautiful,
even though her thyroid
glands have been removed, leaving a slack hollow.

You trot to meet her.
She seats you on a log by the pump.

Masha, their daughter, scampers out naked and hops up beside you.

Her vagina is just a line.
Her eyes are frighteningly steady.

You've learned that well water is heavier than water from a faucet.
Galya turns to heave the bucket at you—
Masha offers soap and you
wash using your hands.
She watches you rub yourself under your swimsuit.

The horns of the storm crack, and Masha squints
at the sky
like a marksman.

It's raining and you're walking on the dirt road
in the direction of Baryatino
when a plaid-scratched Lada pulls over and pins you to the bushes.
The men in the car, leering,
stinking of pivo, yell at you to admit you're

American.
You're scared, but
you won't do it.

You hear the rumble
of his tractor
behind you.
You feel him jump
down to earth
and stride evenly over the uneven field.
He crashes through the messy hedge to face the kulaks.
He hasn't been back from Chechnya a year.

He's closer to your
age than Galya's. You can't figure
out their relationship, by which
you mean you're sure
they don't love each other.

The tractor smells black, like sunflower-seed oil.
The corrugated wheels plough up dust
you can smell dampening
in the rain that rattles
the little windshield.

Your soldier shifts
gears and the tractor shudders.

You go hurtling across the field. The trees joggle
in watercolor at the edges.

When the tractor stops
you think he's going to kiss you. His cheeks
are thin & pitted. But he takes your hand
and places it on the gearshift.

You close your eyes.

The tractor bursts forward.

The sun is combed up through the trees
and the first thing you see when you part
your curtains is Masha sneaking
through the zinnias. Thief, you think,
even as you'd steal her father.

You crawl back under-
neath the mosquito net. You don't bother
tucking it in, the mosquitoes

in your room are nocturnal.
The ones in the woods
are as big as mammals.
Only the first week
did you decline DEET;
now you're a DEET freak
like the rest of them.

Someone's at the door—

Masha.

Her hair bows are bigger than her head.
She wanders toward the mirror, studies herself—

She looks at you in the mirror behind her before she
knocks your perfume over
with the back of her hand.

One of the Andreis in your adult English
class says that the way to tell an American
is if she buys a cigarette lighter
without testing it.
You stand
accused.

At first
you're captivated
by cultural-
seeming facts—

shoes & good teeth.
The way to tell an American,
says Andrei, is when she can't
believe Hermitage admittance
costs more for Americans.
He gets you in his sights.
Have you visited
Hermitage?

Democracy, he continues, is
when everyone gets the same bargain

shoes

good

teeth.

When your adult students in-
vite you on an ex-
pedition to a nearby river, you take your passport
rolled
in your towel.

Seraphima, midforties, with copper hair & male-
pattern baldness,
confides in you: Five years looking for God
and there on Brighton Beach
she saw Him,
taking many

forms along the board-
walk.
Her eyes
shine.

She shows you where to change into your swimsuit in a thicket.
She hangs her bra on a currant bush.

On a day you don't see your soldier
you think he must be avoiding you.

Everything is about you, you accuse yourself.
You eat a dinner of clear soup & moist bread and excuse
yourself.

You've met him before where the farm road ends in field;
there's an inscrutable pile of rocks and you've found
seats with your backs
to the village and smoked
those loose Troika cigarettes.

Tonight the midsummer air is so still

that the smoke just sinks.

The sunset comes in enormous flakes
like shale. You think

you'll remember his name forever

(this is what you can do
in the second
person)

                                but you won't. You can split

yourself in time.
Splitting yourself,
you're both yourself
& your soldier. You
don't know yet that this
is love.

TWELFTH NIGHT

There's a holy stillness one breath before the after-work crowd surges through the door, the leaders of men already calling orders. Bartender! they call him. A G and T Sapphire! Two Absolut martoonies! Shaking peanuts like dice in loose fists, funneling them down their gullets, hoisting coats headed to the mousehole coat check, tossing ties over their shoulders, rubbing the blood back into the keyboards of their hands. You got mine? Grabbing a stool. You got my friend here?

Lucky for everyone, Matthew Evans can take a drink order in each ear, gin in one hand, vodka in the other, he's ambidextrous. Hey! For real, Bartender?

Who doesn't have a duality inside him? Not to mention a rapt multitude.

You got any other tricks? Water to wine, Jesus?

His eyes well with tears.

Gotcha there, he smiles.

Although in his headshots, he's unassuming. Just under six feet, just under forty. A casting agent once told him he was the only male in the western hemisphere who didn't suffer from height inflation. Who knows how it worked in Asia? His leg bones boyishly fumbled into their sockets, his head large and beautifully sculpted. His eyes are wise but also streetwise, knowing danger but not wanting to scare anybody, as if a human were trapped in the body of a shaman's animal.

Unassuming, overall, but with a deep voice like a radio announcer, and a way of smiling sorrowfully behind the bar, averting his eyes when he states, gently, What can I get you. He doesn't pretend it's a question. What balm in this world. You and I, he seems to be saying, are deserving because we know we're undeserving. He'll raise his glass of tap water.

He can practically make his rent on any given after-work Thursday. The thirsty crowd tips flush with clannish pride, like they're hiking their kilts to show off their equipment. Not that anyone's particularly a Scotsman. It was his first audition accent. He was told his smile had a bit of auld lang syne in it.

Then there's a lull, and he'll pause for a moment to look out over that imaginary audience.

How did you get here, Matthew Evans?

How did he get here?

The way almost everybody he knows got to the city.

Youth.

That duplicitous desire of youth for self-knowledge and self-evasion.

His tone is intimate but the acoustics are terrific, to follow a girl, to lose himself, not any girl, his sister, Mary.

He can pull a perfect draught with his eyes closed, pronounce Brouilly, Bourgogne, Châteauneuf-du-Pape without embarrassing anybody. He'd never boast of having traipsed all over Europe. He's never been to Europe. He has a good ear. He's been here. Waiting to be found or to find her.

What if she's behind him—now? He's on his way to work. He whips around on the sidewalk.

What if that's her, ten people ahead in a line at the bookstore two days before Christmas? He gives up his place. The line fills in like water.

Sometimes when you feel your going
Would leave an unfillable hole
Just follow this simple instruction
And see how it humbles your soul.

Take a bucket and fill it with water
Put your hand in up to the wrist
Pull it out and the hole remaining
Is a measure of how you'll be missed.

That's the poem his mother presented him with when he left for the city.

His face is not symmetrical, but expressive, as a mother's face is to her child. No stranger to suffering, but absent self-pity. When he rests his hip against the bar and asks, sideways, What's it like out there? Or, Plans for the weekend? People feel he could fill in, if they're short on love, or friendship. He has a longstanding policy that whoever stumps him with a drink drinks on him for the duration.

The restaurant is at the elbow of one of those Village alleys. He's seen it through the last three incarnations. Crescendo Café, Kristos' Place, Parker's. He can recall elegantly bored coat-check girls, German or Italian students from whom, in fact, he still receives postcards, and he can bring to mind delicate, swaggering, subaltern busboys, a tall and haughty Berber who lorded it over them. The season that cappuccinos first swept the nation, the nation being New York City, a neighbor-hood girl was hired to handle the froth. It turned out she was the punk-rock daughter of a famous civil rights lawyer.

There were cameo appearances: Shel Silverstein, dressed for Key West down to the white sandals, David and Joyce Dinkins. Olympia Dukakis with a queen's bearing, looking exactly like she did in *Moonstruck*. The entire cast of *Tony and Tina's Wedding* drank Heineken. The inimitable Turturro siblings. An extremely shy writer might have been Thomas Pynchon.

Passersby under peach-colored streetlights, the Jamaican lady with a hat made of fruit and flowers, the Gay Pride parade, the sense of Cyndi Lauper a continuous reel. A slim homosexual with that strange homo combo of diffidence and predation—I saw you from the street, he suggested. Matthew hated to disappoint him. Yes, Matthew takes it seriously, the edict about staying in one spot in the forest. In the last, well, almost two decades, Mary could have found him here almost any evening.

A table? A beverage?

He's an actor, he admits, if pressed. Everyone looks for him—for the rest of their lives—in plays and movies.

Occasionally he runs with the before-work crowd along the river. He nods to Lady Liberty, island prisoner. Six in the morning, the water hurrying to shore. A lanky banker and his feathered retriever. An old dude in a Guinea tee, nickel-colored arms. Matthew would stretch but he's tired of being hit on.

A disco ball breaks in a big bare tree and a thousand birds open the branches. A disheveled hawk perched in another tree—he and Mary always used to take the hawk's side in the forest. Mary was going to be a soloist. The last time he saw her, as if this were the root cause, was the night before the high school–band trip to the city.

Months of bake sales to raise money: marshmallow snowmen and cupcakes with Reese's Cups baked into their centers, study halls spent lettering Magic-Marker banners. Band members flipping porkpie hats, their noses too big for their faces. People gave more to the drama club. Girls with raccoon eyeliner and pretty boys like Matthew in tight Brando T-shirts.

Was she wearing her band uniform in the morning? Or just jeans and a sweatshirt big enough to disappear in? Her toothbrush was gone. It was the last time he wept in front of his mother.

Memory is like a silent movie. When he's alone in his apartment, he puts music to it. The big-band numbers she played by ear on her trumpet.

He remembers the stricken music teacher, Mr. Rothko, his robust hips and little round glasses, who lost his union card as a result of losing Mary. Five years until he was hired half-time by a parochial school. Or so they heard.

Matthew told the detective they had different friends, he and his sister. Their mother was always on Mary about it. But their mother never suggested Matthew make friends with Black people.

Here are his professional headshots, his truly sea-blue eyes, Can you play a gay guy, Mr. Evans?

His clothes are loose and baggy, he could be changing bodies underneath them.

You'd prefer to play a hero? says the acid young director. The straight-guy Friday? The coy and show-stealing butler?

In any case, thinks Matthew, he's supposed to be a cipher, not a celebrity. He's supposed to be Everyman. Everywhere, he sees Mary.

Foam of dark hair, small body like a cricket. Chalky, old lady's elbows.

Okay, headshots, but let's play around for a minute. The photographer hands him a pair of suspenders.

Stretching them, clowning, he says in his passable brogue, I came after a girl called Mary. The photographer is a woman in a sack dress. He has the sense that it covers her face, too, with eyeholes.

Look at me like you're looking at yourself in the mirror, says the photographer.

Matthew squints at the camera's dark nozzle.

He used to think he'd run into her in a midtown lunch place. The same kind of place a traveling high school band would take over. He used to imagine people turning from their companions or their coleslaw in slow motion, the atmospheric coffee, the ding of the bell in the kitchen when the food was up—working in restaurants you could never not hear that.

Hey waitress-cleaning-your-nails-like-a-cat. Look up! He and Mary used to chase each other up trees like squirrels.

What did they say to each other when they played they were lost in the forest? Which was their main game, their whole childhood.

You're supposed to let the search party do the circling. You're the tree. You are so much the tree that they pass right by you—even the dogs, all riled up, scatterbrained and twitching.

I came looking for my sister.

You know any jokes, Bartender?

Sure, the punchline of female anatomy. One woman in a thousand has a double uterus. Maybe it's a million. Their mother is twice the woman. Twice the trouble befalls her.

Woman duped by womb! Twenty-five cents to see the twins of different races!

You know any stories?

Once upon a time in a small town on Long Island, Linda Reilly boarded the train to the city. She had a notion to buy a Christmas coat, a coat for herself for Christmas.

Their mother, Linda Reilly. She was twenty-two, firm waist and swishy hair, teaching first grade, possessed by a desire for a coat that no other young lady was already wearing.

A magic coat. Cut from a flying carpet. Something she could wear with glass slippers, any fairy tale would do, she spent the morning window shopping among other starry-eyed window shoppers. But then maybe her dream coat wasn't in season, maybe she was ahead of the times, maybe behind them. In any case, she couldn't find what she wanted, and footsore, finally, around lunchtime, she wandered out of the Christmas crowds to find a lunch place. She sat down at the counter with one seat between her and a soldier whose back she'd seen—she liked the easy forward angle—through the window.

Pheromonic convergence. That's one way to describe the meeting. Their mother tipping forward to match him, eyeing him, ordering coffee—

She'd been hungry but now she wasn't. The soldier seemed surprised and pleased. It's good coffee, he said faithfully.

It was clear that neither one of them had ever been to the lunch place. It put them on equal footing. He was on leave. What war? laughed Linda. He was stationed in Italy. He was coaxing his ma down from the tree of his disappearance. Linda laughed again—his way with words, his devotion to his mother. They moved from the counter to a table in the window. The afternoon hours never touched the ground. You're a poet! said Linda.

They split a sandwich. He handed her one of the toothpicks with the tiny red flags. She spun it between her thumb and finger. Hours and hours, but it seemed as if they each only said a single sentence. Their words to each other were that perfect.

No one bothered them. The thing Linda liked about the city was that there was no wrong time for anything. Lunch, coffee, talk to a Black man.

The following Saturday he was already holding a table. Holding a table! You're strong! She was lightheaded. Love was a concussion, or a corset. He said he wasn't going back over. He wasn't in the habit of saying what he meant but with her there was no sense being guarded. The world was guarded against them. He glanced once around the lunch place and then eased her ginger hair over her shoulders.

Wasn't hair supposed to be dead, like fingernails? But she could feel him with it. She closed her eyes and she could feel the silk of his feeling.

Linda Reilly turned twenty-three. She couldn't exactly say they were dating. He hadn't asked her. He was playing his trumpet on off nights at a bar partly owned by his uncle or his cousin or—Could she come? He stopped saying much about what he was doing during the daylight hours when Linda conducted her first-graders.

Blink and you'd miss it: A loss of heart? Just a stupid misunderstanding? Two weeks in a row Linda sat by herself at the counter. The lunch place hummed and clattered around her. You waiting for that soldier? said the waitress. Not unkindly, but with no real confidence, either. It wasn't Linda's pride that was hurt but her heart, she realized with wonder.

She skipped a week. She went back one last Saturday but she couldn't bear to sit down. She paced the sidewalk for an hour, feeling crazy.

She was a lovely girl of marriageable age and she had a marriage prospect. One of the sons of Evans Construction. She had known all the sons forever. They were getting all the contracts in Suffolk and in Nassau counties. Linda Reilly and Jim Evans were married.

Jim took a promotion from his father and traveled to Detroit to scout new equipment. Dozers and dumps, he told her. She should stay with his parents. Shouldn't lift a finger, in her condition. Although at six weeks, she wasn't showing.

Anyone who's ever heard a story could see this one coming: Linda on the train to the city. She just wanted to sit in the lunch place. There were two pale spider plants in the window with their dozens of air babies. She wouldn't have known how to find him, anyway. She just wanted to sit at the counter and pretend she was waiting. Pretend he would come up behind her, and as if to steal an extra moment, she'd see him in the big faux-gilt-framed mirror a moment before he said, Linda.

Had the soldier had the same thought exactly? On that fateful Saturday? It's hard for Matthew to believe it. Matthew doesn't think men are like that—telepathic, or, for that matter, sentimental. His own father, Jim Evans, sure wasn't.

She was pregnant. The best birth control on the planet.

Their mother's double body gave birth like the separate taps for hot and cold water, only Mary was the color of the lashing gray ocean.

He knows the big Evans family, you can't help knowing them in the town he's from and all the towns around it. But he's never come face-to-face with Jim, his father.

Mary hadn't come home with the band, they'd waited through Christmas, they'd dragged the forest, even though she was last seen in New York City. Evans Construction had a plan for the forest, so the draggers had doubled as surveyors, and investors.

He couldn't lie when the detective asked was his sister happy.

This honeysuckle is pulling the fence down! raged their mother. Bare of leaves, they could see how it pried the slats apart.

But now she was just his mother. She scuffed and kicked at one of the honeysuckle stitches. She bent down and tried to tug a ropey end from the half-frozen earth. Like pulling a suture before the wound has healed. Stretch marks like rope burn. Earth came with it.

The trees come out in body bags after dark, after Christmas, and leave dark stains on the sidewalks. He gets home from work and the snow by the door of his building is two slain sentries.

He's barefoot in his apartment. His feet are simple genius, like Shaker furniture.

His answering-machine light is blinking.

Soon there were thousands of blinking lights in place of the forest.

If she wanted to she could find him.

There's a mrawling from the yard below and Matthew goes to the back window of his apartment. A girl in his building lets her tomcat spend the night fighting. He's hurried past her without looking up on several occasions. He doesn't want to be the resident curmudgeon, but the tom sprays, and the old brick is a sponge. The whole building smells like the girl's hit-man tomcat.

He presses the answering-machine button and it's Althea. It's a great name. It adds character not just to her but to everything. Her voice is too loud against the bare floors of his apartment. He may be too old for her but she seems to like the idea of the old-fashioned as in timeless barman.

Know any jokes? she still asks him.

His humor is earned, but not burnished. A man walks into a bar.

Okay, she prompts him.

Spread on the bar, his hands look like neat handwriting. Not his, he's a sprawling lefty who endured reparative therapy to make him right again. A man walks into a bar, he says again, pauses.

So? says Althea.

He sends a rag out over the polished surface with a half smile.

117

Althea, childlike in anticipation, is waiting.

Ouch, says Matthew.

It takes her a moment.

He likes how they met, how she got up and carried her plate over to the bar; a weary busboy followed with her napkin. She told Matthew he reminded her of a certain sensitive actor whose name she could never remember.

Her martini glass had a meniscus and dry sides when he placed it before her, but she couldn't get it to her lips without spilling. He was swiping with a bar mop before she even finished her swallow. She said, Oh. She paused. I like that. They smiled unarmed at each other for a moment.

Gin, vodka, vodka, gin, vodka—the pattern of total orders just slightly favors vodka.

It's three thirty in the morning. He returns Althea's call anyway. Her outgoing message to the world: Do I know you?

It becomes her. Matthew always has the urge to leave his message in disguise. It's what she wants, isn't it? *Do I know you?* It's Althea's way of taking control of the fact that she lives with seven million strangers.

How would he describe her? First of all, California. A little bit heavy, comfortable, as his mother used to say, but sleek like a porpoise. She's half Danish, or so she says—he's never considered the Danes a distinctive people—with a glossy bob the color of redwood. Thanksgiving he drove to California to meet her stepmother, who is her only extant family. She talks like she killed them off, but it's a cover for her sadness. She took him to a park where he had the opportunity to drive his car through the giant, upended cross section of a redwood. Redwoods are the dinosaurs of the tree world, read the sign, your contribution can help prevent their extinction. Matthew stuck a five-dollar bill in the varnished wood coffin.

Instead of flying back separately, Althea drove with him cross country. She talked a lot about her childhood. He listened. Doing something toward love is better than doing nothing.

She scoured their lives for people they might have in common. At first he thought it was her way of getting to know him, sweet and quirky. But then she seemed almost desperate about it, and superstitious. As if it were coincidence itself that would bind them, bless their union. As if without coincidence Matthew would be a perennial stranger.

After twenty-six years on the planet, she said, she didn't want to start all over. He laughed at her. Twenty-six! There has to be some karmic *something*, she said, begging the universe.

Then, after several weeks of coming up with nothing, she said flatly, We're starting a new lineage. She wasn't pleased about it.

She's an event coordinator. She cooks carelessly but contentedly, and she doesn't believe in cleaning up till the next morning. When they're finished she sidles close to him on the sofa with her photo albums. She has that after dinner effect on him: he'll do anything.

He's seen baby pictures and summer car camping. He's seen fifth-grade Disneyland and sixth-grade Yosemite. Her parents' funerals. He's said the right things, or close enough. Tonight we have Althea Takes New York, says Althea.

There's the trusty Pathfinder that got her across the country, there she is in her roadworn University of Colorado sweatpants. And no, for the record, Matthew knows absolutely no one from Colorado, a one-airport state, he's pretty sure; he'd be hard pressed to name the capital city, or the airport.

She weights his arm across her shoulders like a beanbag doorsnake. Those things that keep the drafts out. Here she is with her coworkers at a restaurant, red-eye like taillights, she points people out to him, and Ah, he says, when he recognizes someone they've talked about. She does a puppy wriggle.

He feels lulled by his single glass of wine—he doesn't drink, normally—and he senses, gratefully, that Althea might even be getting tired. He could stay or he could go home, tonight; he's grateful, too, to be at the point in the relationship where either is acceptable. Close to love, maybe, but savoring the approach a little longer.

There's a series of snapshots that chronicles a trip to the supermarket. Althea laughs. She almost forgot they did that, she and Deirdre. You know, she says, after college? You feel like why isn't my trip to the supermarket some witty art film? Wittgenstein? Was he the filmmaker? Matthew has no idea. Let's see if you can guess what we're having for dinner from the pictures, says Althea. Dutifully Matthew takes the photo album onto his lap for closer inspection. Inside D'Agostino's, individual pictures of all the ingredients, like supporting actors.

Althea has large, still eyes, and it occurs to him that she abuses her loneliness. Matthew turns the page. As if her loneliness were a starving dog she kept chained in the basement. But now she's following her pictorial history avidly. There's a shot of the checkout girl, a coffee-and-cream sixteen-year-old, examining the credit card, the strip must be scratched, she's going to have to punch in all those numbers. Her dark hair is glazed into a ponytail. Weird, thinks Matthew, to have a picture of a stranger in your photo album. Almost creepy. He feels sorry for the girl at the checkout. He can read her gold script necklace: Marisa. Another frame: Marisa hands back the credit card. Her face is shockingly open. Has she seen the camera? Matthew thinks he will go home tonight. Whenever, in fact, he can smoothly exit.

Finally, Althea and Deirdre are leaving D'Agostino's, but Jesus, it's really too fetishy for Matthew. They're posing, tourists in front of a monument, a monument to themselves, they've asked a stranger to click, each girl with two plastic grocery bags cinched in each fist, like egg sacs, their heads inclined toward each other. They look an awful lot alike, actually—how had he missed that fact that they're dressed identically? Jeans, boots, black T-shirts with glittery stripes horizontal across their stocky torsos.

Now the camera looks straight at the exit. All that rubber around the automatic folding doors, like the soft black muzzle of a horse, thinks Matthew.

He turns the page. There's one last picture. The camera has caught someone entering as Althea and Deirdre exit. Matthew doesn't even have to look closely. He doesn't have to change his position on the sofa. *I came looking for my sister.* He is looking straight into the twin brown eyes of his sister Mary.

What if it weren't true? The coffee, the counter, Linda Reilly and the Black soldier? It had never occurred to Matthew that Mary wasn't proof of love, and proof of its loss. But if it weren't true—their mother's love affair, the lunch place—then there was another story.

He goes to turn on the shower. Innumerable spiders seem to have hatched across the ceiling. Invisible webs. Untethered. Is he supposed to pretend they're not there and just turn on the water?

An old guy orders a Bob Dandy. Just to humor him, Matthew scratches his head, wonders aloud, Now what goes into that one?

He looks off into the distance. He's campy at heart. He's playing a part—always. To make everyone feel special, seen.

Althea wants to try what's left in the shaker. In the squares of her pupils Matthew finds his own reflections.

She's wearing a vintage tweed suit the color of a Tootsie Roll. A fox collar. The skirt is short enough to show her chubby knees, she might have taken the hem up. The cropped jacket is tight across the bust; in fact, she looks gorgeous.

He pours out the shaker in a wineglass. A beautiful redwood, for Althea.

I have a proposition, says Althea. She makes these little games up. You, darling, are to disguise yourself. She winks at Bob Dandy. It's extremely simple.

She explains that she has one shot to go up to the right person on the subway platform. If she doesn't recognize him, Matthew is to board the train without her.

There it is—she invites her loneliness, invents his betrayal.

Bob Dandy politely requests a cherry. Matthew passes him a bread plate of maraschino cherries, probably ten, like crimson, waxen olives. He thinks, it can't be a costume that looks like a costume.

Althea is watching him intently. He catches her at it and she flashes him a smile.

Too obvious to dress like a woman. In any case, Althea will probably be looking for him to be a woman. He hasn't told her about Mary—neither his sister's existence, nor the fact that she has a cameo in Althea's photo album. Althea would claim it turned her on, if he dressed like a woman.

I'm good for his acting, says Althea to Bob Dandy.

No mustache, sunglasses. No boom box or attaché case. If he were a type, she could say, and read into it like some ten-dollar astrologist, A Wall Street lawyer! Well then what are you doing behind a bar, loser?

Recognition is an aphrodisiac, Althea is saying. I guess I'll take a Bob Dandy, since you're mixing them, Barman.

Just once, in almost two decades, he went up to the wrong person. Night, starry lights in the black fountain in the gleaming plaza of Lincoln Center. He'd sat through a jazz concert. The trumpet was a grotesque white man—heavy, stunted, little piggish eyes and a low forehead.

A skinny girl in a cap was standing with her back to him before the fountain. She wore black leggings and motorcycle boots, one of those bomber jackets from a show. As he got closer, he saw the embroidered "Alvin Ailey." So, a dancer. Of course! His heart skipped like a record, fast-forwarded like a cassette tape—he forced himself to slow down, he had to be sure it was Mary.

It was as if he were looking inside himself to recognize her. Mary!

She turned around.

His first impression was that there was no face at all. His own face must have showed his horror for the girl threw up the hood underneath her company jacket and strode off toward the busy lights and traffic of Broadway.

Their agreement was that Althea would say his name when she found him. Hide-and-seek among human disguises. *Matthew.* She had to commit herself. When she said his name the game was over. No testing: Do you have the time? while doing a preliminary once-over. If she got it wrong, Matthew would get on the next train. Without indication. God, that was depressing. That was the dark and bully side of Althea.

They had decided on West Fourth Street. As he dropped underground he could hear ungainly violin music, someone sawing away at a partita for quarters, the same phrase over and over. It occurred to Matthew that Althea had commissioned the musician in order to create some kind of heightened experience. An *event.* Her métier, she called it. Matthew made his way down the platform. He wore hefty tan Carhartts, big blond boots, a hard hat. His T-shirt was dirty. In fact he could see in his mind's eye the Evans Construction logo. No tool belt, though, no mini cooler.

If only a splash of spare change would shut the busker up instead of fortify him. As Matthew got closer he saw the chapped face of an outdoor alcoholic. Matthew placed a dollar in the butterflied violin case and immediately regretted it. The hack had to stop playing, reach down and secure his money. When he started up again, it was to serenade Matthew.

He waited. He wondered if anyone noticed he let the trains come and go without him. When he finally saw Althea on the stairs, it was nearly an hour later than the time they'd agreed on. He might have been annoyed but there was something in her careful walk that stopped him. It occurred to him that she was giving him time to get here. He felt almost sick imagining her anticipation.

He ambled toward her. The idea wasn't to hide, certainly. He saw that her eyes were red and her face was puffy from crying. Something had clearly happened. This wasn't in the script. Should he be the one to break the spell, cut, as it were, the bullshit? Because that's what it was, and he couldn't believe he was down here in a glorified sewer hoping to be recognized by heart in metaphorical darkness. Jesus. You couldn't choreograph coincidence. It was a cheap fairy tale, coincidence; not the logic of destiny. Why hadn't he seen that?

Just as he was going to say her name she began purposefully toward an old lady seated on a bench underneath the staircase. The crone had a gauzy purple kerchief over her head and beads falling through her fingers.

Two props; plus hospital shoes, and a face like an aerial view of the wrinkled Rocky Mountains. Her state, Colorado. A Black woman, come on, how did Althea think he could achieve that? He wasn't an actor with a staff of makeup artists.

Just like they'd agreed, Althea spoke. Matthew?

The old lady didn't even look up from her counting. So accustomed to crazies, crazy herself, talking to God, God bless her. He watched Althea wait for him to emerge from the costume. At least her face looked a little less blotchy. He watched her wonder if he was prolonging the suspense, masterfully.

Then—and this part did seem choreographed, even destined—headlamp-first, a train swam up out of the darkness.

It engaged with the platform, and Matthew took one sideways step onto it. Althea didn't even have time to look around, make other guesses.

He didn't call her. She didn't call him, either. It seemed like she should have called because it was her game, and finally, he felt used by it. Days went by, then a week. She didn't show up at the restaurant; he never saw her pass by outside on the sidewalk.

He had slipped the picture of Mary entering D'Agostino's out of the plastic pocket of Althea's photo album. He couldn't quite shake the feeling of having jinxed Althea's experiment. He carried the picture around with him in one book or another—it didn't fit in his wallet. He took it out a dozen times over the course of an evening, held it below the lip of the bar, his own backstage. He took it out on the subway home again.

In fact, any sense he had of her, Mary, disappeared when he looked too closely. When he looked too closely she was any, as white people said, half-Black thirty-seven-year-old woman with big brown eyes and a cosmopolitan Afro. She could be an extra. Just a look of: What am I going to pick up for dinner?

The first week of April, he's walking across town, west to east, from the restaurant. He has a part in a graduate-student production of *Twelfth Night*. Which part? Of course, Sebastian. The long-lost brother. *Twelfth Night*—he's reading it for the first time—takes a lot of stories to make up one story. Like anything in nature, a close-up of a flower, bubbles in a bottled soda, skin at the cellular level.

Something he's never done—he's taking off work for evening rehearsals. Of course he's not getting paid, but the truth is he's not a starving artist, he's a rather flush bartender. Tonight's rehearsal is going to be practically under the FDR trusses. There's a strip of park along the river, the graduate-student director assured him, but Matthew wants to lay eyes on it before the rehearsal.

The restaurant isn't open till noon, but he had a cup of coffee with the kitchen and finished the wine inventory. Angelo scrambled a couple of eggs for him. Dislocating not to come in tonight. He tries not to read into it. It could be the beginning of something or it could be—nothing. He takes comfort from the fact that Angelo doesn't really care: just so long as his salad prep or his dishwasher doesn't play hooky. Bartender? Just another white guy, says Angelo good-naturedly.

He passes a small park he's never noticed. Is there a chance he's never actually walked this city block, never chosen this stretch above all others? Since when did he presume to have covered every block in the city?

The park is elevated, like a stage, although obscured by scaly sycamores. Probably built on a heap of nineteenth century garbage. There are five or six steps leading up to the iron gate, and it seems that there's something slightly off about it. A movie crew somewhere? Strange light, like an inverted halo.

Is it a park within a park, for instance? He laughs at himself. Too much Shakespeare.

A single person is sitting on a bench eating a sandwich. Slight and girlish, with a sympathetic tip to her balletic neck, thin-as-shell shoulders. Her dark hair is combed and twisted with a big plastic clip from the hairdresser's. Fat pigeons nod and coo around her.

She seems at once misplaced, and familiar. Before he thinks it through, Matthew starts toward her.

It takes him only an instant to realize. He watches her look up and do the same double take, but there's nothing now except to complete the approach, they're the only two people—as is if they're the only two people in the entire city.

This scene is going to be a real clunker.

Reluctantly, she places her bread roll on its waxed paper and stands to meet him. They have given themselves away, and now they mirror each other's disappointment.

Is it Tanya? says Matthew, as generously as he can muster. She nods, barely. She gestures up toward one of the flatfaced office buildings that rise around the park.

This is where I work, says Tanya.

There are a few leggy rosebushes with a few yellow leaves that have hung on through the whole winter. The sycamores in a row are especially drab: the pigeons of the tree world. The confetti of green that's sprinkled elsewhere, in April—this forgotten park is in a canyon of cold skyscrapers.

Up close, her eyes are wet, glittery. Adult braces. He thinks they are a great distance from the apartment building where they are both tenants.

If you don't mind, says Tanya, waving apologetically at her sandwich.

Sure, says Matthew. It comes out as if he were a petulant god disappointed in his own creation. She sits back down on the bench and takes a half-hearted bite. She's probably the kind of woman who hates to be watched while she's eating. Could he even claim they have an acquaintanceship? He knows she's single, like he is, and with undue ire he realizes suddenly that she flaunts it by keeping that tomcat with dark circles under his eyes who hunts all night in the basement. Takes his brawls out to the back garden. Matthew's apartment, too, smells of rank, skulky tomcat. Had he caught himself quicker, he would never, of course, have crossed the park to meet Tanya Varga.

She's younger than he is, to start with. Even younger than Althea? Clear skin, a nondrinker. Overly devoted to nephews and nieces. She has cheap rings on every one of her fingers: gold plate, rhinestone. A tiny, frayed piece of deli turkey on her dressfront. On her breast, actually. Someone could find something erotic about it.

I'm sorry about that cat, says Tanya.

Matthew raises an eyebrow.

My old roommate finally came and got him.

I didn't know you had a cat, Matthew hears himself saying.

Oh, says Tanya, relieved, her plentiful mouth relaxing into a smile. I thought all the neighbors hated me.

Her eyes are actually kind of flashy. Green? If she were his type, she'd be beautiful. Now what does that mean? Well, the marine-blue twinset, the stockings that come in a plastic egg from the drugstore—his mother wore them. How pathetic, really, about the tomcat. Living in fear of her neighbors.

He laughs rather fraternally. Saying he never hated her is not the point. Embarrassingly not the point. But what is the replacement point?

He says, See you back at the ranch, Tanya.

Okay, she says, gamely.

Of course, now he'll probably run into her on a daily basis. He walks uptown for a while, in some consternation. Beautiful—if he were another man—Jesus. That was the way he used to feel about Mary. Is that why he aspires to be an actor? If he weren't Matthew?

He remembers their mother winding up, slamming a magazine against the table. Do you two ever enjoy a moment of silence? Be quiet, oh please be quiet! She sank to her knees before them. It had shocked them and they were quiet. Then she got on with cooking dinner. And he remembers her saying to him in private, Now Matt, you'll look out for her at school, won't you? And then, No one should have to apologize just for being a girl, said their mother, so untruthfully that Matthew felt momentarily disembodied.

She was capable though, Mary, toting her trumpet between the buildings in the middle-school complex. When he told her—bragging, to get her attention—that their mother had charged him with her protection, Mary shut him off with the hard angle of her shoulder.

Matthew glances around him. He's overshot his cross street. How did that happen? And he doesn't have the book he was carrying. The book he left his apartment with this morning, left the restaurant with, in which he'd slid the picture of Mary. His heart races. He forces himself to stop and open his backpack. He knows it's not going to be there, and it's not. He turns around and starts jogging.

This time the park is empty—of books and of people.

A small wind comes up and the sycamores make accommodations in their empty branches. He remembers, suddenly, clearly, how he set his book down on this rim of cement, this half-wall—he touches it—as he was talking to Tanya.

The next day, she's spitting mail from her mailbox into the trash can when Matthew enters their building. She looks up from her sorting. Hi, Hi, they overlap each other.

No love letters? says Matthew.

They're breaking down my door, says Tanya.

Right. Matthew laughs in spite of himself. Of course she's the desperate-for-a-husband type of twenty-five-year-old.

Her hair is down—she looks even younger. Fine dark hair, cinnamon where the sun's touched it. You didn't by chance—they've spoken in perfect unison. They look at each other in astonishment.

You didn't—she starts, and he accidentally interrupts her—Did you—She holds up her hand. Her enormous pie eyes are laughing. Pie eyes! What their mother used to call Mary's. A book? she manages.

Matthew doesn't dare speak. He nods. She has a big knotty shoulder bag and she reaches into it and produces his book. He doesn't dare page through it for the picture. In private. But now—he's not sure if he can move past her. He's not sure that if he starts she won't start too, in unison. He bunches forward. He opens the inner door, holds it open.

Her braces are like the metal from an unfolded paper clip. Girls used to do that—before they were old enough to get set up with orthodontics. Is she going to that geometric hull that rises above a dingy little park with flaking sycamores? It's Saturday. But he works, later. On other days, does she have to eat her sandwich standing up because a bum has bedded down on her park bench? He's sort of sweating. Or is she heading up-stairs, like he is, to her one-man show, excuse me, one-woman? He's still holding the door for her, if she wants it.

Oh. Go ahead, she says. I'll be a minute.

All right, he tucks his tail for his own benefit, playacting, as if he were this hopeful pup, in love, like the guys he faces every night on his barstools.

He skips stairs on the way up to his apartment. What's that? Something under the door, a folded piece of notebook paper. His own heart hammering? He puts his hand on his heart, this is crazy. What's going on here? It's from Tanya. It must be. It's the love letter he just teased her about. He's certain of it. He snatches the paper up and jabs it in his inside pocket. He bounds back down the stairs but the entryway, foy-er, vestibule, what do you call it, is empty.

She's already halfway down the block, past the useless shoe-repair shop, past the pay phone with the phone always dangling out of its holster, clattering around the pole soldered into the sidewalk.

Tanya! he calls, starting after her. He has to run to catch up to her. She stops and turns toward him. Her eyes are lit up with the new greens and yellows.

He holds out the folded paper.

Her eyes are shining. I wanted you to know—

You found my book, he finishes for her. Still, he unfolds the paper. If he could take his eyes off her he'd read it.

V-J DAY

In August the manhole covers began to seep. Summer had the same texture as the local Eyewitness news, thought Sonia. A section of highway had crumbled in the heat like a biscuit. A tragic fire in a condemned Woonsocket warehouse where a boy and girl, five and three, had been sleeping. In a reddish photo they were looking up like shelter puppies from a bare mattress. "It appears their parents had problems related to homelessness," said the female newscaster, as if she hated to say it, her voice, her instrument, full of regret, but also recrimination. "There's Lorenzo—" She had to wait out the wind in her mic. The girl filled the screen to the very edges. "Her little name was Amy."

The same wind raised a thin wing of the newscaster's hair and you could see behind her the blackened, gutted warehouse. Key change. "It's V-J Day here in Rhode Island—"

Sonia called upstairs, "Boys? Are you ready?"

The wind was conducting the giant manes of the street trees, stirring them every which-way. Her husband had said she should stay in the house; she loved the house, he told the mediator. All those years she had staunchly kept to herself her dismay at 748 Weymouth, and now, when she tried to protest, he sucked his teeth thoughtfully. "You've always had a strange sense of yourself, Sonia." How did men learn this trick? To make strange someone's knowledge of herself in order to justify their failure to know her. He promptly installed himself in a riverview condominium.

The boys ducked wordlessly into the car. The air conditioner blasted heat for the first five minutes.

Outside the office supply store there was some nature so denatured it didn't know how to ask for rain. The doors shuddered and parted. Right away there were specials on mini staplers and pencil pouches and caramel-nut bars. Sonia's sons drifted off and then popped up in the aisles of phones and touches, but mid-divorce they wouldn't ask for anything, not even a gadget. They were like Diana's sons, navy blue and blond and brass, mute, mysterious.

She filled the demi cart with three-ring binders. She put her hand out to stop the slack-bodied employee so white, under the glaring lights, he was lilac.

"Do you know where I'd find a graphing calculator?" She fell in step behind him. He gestured vaguely, then left her alone to study the clamshell packages.

The parking lot stuck to their shoes when they crossed the grid back to the car. Hot wind ballooned into plastic shopping bags and lifted them into trees like cheap bamboo back scratchers. Her sons spread out; it wouldn't have been clear the three of them were together.

The specialty running store was on a treeless thoroughfare of car washes and nightclubs. She parked on the street. The wind would blow the air off the face of the earth, she said in general.

Her older son had taught himself to raise an eyebrow.

There was a young soldier next to them on the padded bench trying on Adidas. They waited for their salesman to bring up the boxes. He was the same age as the soldier, only with long hair and the slight build of a doe. He paused to assess the gait of a barelegged boy trotting down the section of track you could try your new shoes on.

"Busy this morning," said Sonia mildly.

"V-J Day." She caught his darting glance at the soldier. Theirs was the only state that observed the holiday. "An excuse for slaughter," he said, bowing to lace the shoes with quick, expert motions. He took a knee to help her son stick his foot in.

The soldier was quiet.

Sonia's paternal grandfather had been an ambulance driver in World War II; her mother's father had been too old to serve, had stayed home with his daughters. White males, whales, she pronounced silently, but that was in insult to her mammal kin, the beluga whale at the Mystic Aquarium who nursed her single calf for a decade. White males had a harder time with divorce, at least statistically, her friend Ruth had told her. The shame of canned food, hand-washing single dishes. But either despite the shame or because of it, Sonia's husband was now more central to his own life than ever. In his absence, she found herself considering all the things she'd never done, she said to Ruth, like be a Supreme Court justice, one of the finest jobs available to women.

Why was she so chippy? As if her inner life was one of those shouty reruns, a manufactured, mean-girl mentality.

The mediator's office was in the same metal building as the campaign headquarters of the female candidate for governor. Spray-on carpet had been applied to the walls and the floors; you had to use a communal key for the restroom. With the mediator present, her husband had said that it was because he could no longer make her smile. For a moment, she was stunned by his sneakiness. Then she tried to smile and found that indeed she couldn't. "You got my best years," said her husband.

The mediator looked like clergy, his eggshell chin tucked into his collar. She suspected their sinless case bored him. He was white like they were but because he was gay he could go home to his partner and say, over his reading glasses, "White people problems." She imagined a preening silence.

She was a middle-school English teacher. Twelve percent of her students met grade-level expectations in literacy, eight percent in math. There were schools in the district that did even worse. Her goal for them was that they fall in love with one book over the course of middle school, even *Captain Underpants*, and write one cool sentence. The last five minutes of every period she just covered her ears. "What you say, Miss???" they called out to her.

She insisted she wasn't depressed; she just lacked energy.

The clergyman pressed his lips together. "Come on, Sonia," said her husband. Why, if he was divorcing her, was her husband still allowed to dislike her?

She wondered if the mediator rented his office by the hour. Not a picture on the wall, not even a diploma from an online university.

A building like this could be folded flat and sold back for scrap metal. The carpet burned off with a blowtorch. Somewhat to her horror—not horror, it was satisfaction—it was the same building to which she'd once delivered an anonymous letter. She'd crept down these same underlit hallways, trying to figure out how to hand the hot evidence to his secretary. An older girl, a junior in high school, had convinced her then-seventh-grade son to walk out of a liquor store with a bottle of wine, in exchange for a certain sexual favor. He'd grabbed his hair in agony confessing and Sonia could see his scalp stretching. Then his soft face was pumping heat before tears: "Am I going to go to jail?"

Did he not sense her boundaries? Did he have no respect for his mother's innocence?

"Tell me the name of that girl," she'd said finally.

The girl's father—Google, that guts-spiller—was a low-rent CPA, also an organizer for the local 5K for breast cancer. Boob-a-thons, her husband called them.

"Dear Mr. Vitti. Writing an anonymous letter is by far one of the strangest things I've done as mother, but I wanted you to know that your daughter may have a drinking problem."

It had felt so good to throw it at him, this unknown father, to lash out, especially as she posed as fair minded. "I'm writing because I would want to know if it was one of mine—"

Her husband had played it cool. "There's going to come a time when he'll regret leaving that blow job on the table."

She dropped the boys back home and drove on—she was having lunch with Ruth and Elena. Elena worked for the state historical society and had the Monday holiday.

Ruth said it was common for the estranged wife to want to rescue the husband.

"Really?"

"Oh I don't know," said Ruth, and they all laughed.

She didn't know if Ruth's and Elena's grandfathers had served. It wasn't the kind of thing women asked each other. Imagine: they had six grandfathers between them. Half a dozen young men, a squad, a task force.

She confessed she was taking a little extra thyroid to brighten her personality, to prove she still cared, and Elena looked worried. Ruth rolled her eyes: "Try whiskey." If only she were not herself but either one of them. Ruth had got her divorce out of the way ten years ago and was leaner and funnier because of it; Elena and Tim were inviolable, dear Tim, an honorary woman.

She drove home through the poorer part of the city. There was a rattletrap Toyota angled onto the curb under an overpass, an uncertain array of matching Buddhist monks wandering around the casualty. Across the road under the low wing of the off-ramp heroin ghouls eyed the men in yellow robes. She drove carefully between the factions.

She pulled into the parking spot that the Realtor, long ago, had had the nerve to call a driveway. The back half of the car obstructed the sidewalk. No neighbor had ever complained, which she appreciated more than ever now that she was single. She would have to remind her royal sons to wheel out the trash. The house next door was owned by a Chinese family, which made her feel like a full participant in the species. There was a fake flower cone, an autumnal cornucopia, on the front door. All the blinds stayed closed, but Sonia could see from her bedroom a subtle glow in an upstairs window which at first she'd thought meant someone was Skyping, or shopping for sale sweaters, but now she imagined as a terrarium. The two houses shared a streetlight that flooded the block with crimelessness.

Lately they'd put up a sign in front in Chinese, with a phone number. It had surprised her. "I guess they're appealing to their countrymen," she'd said drily to Princess Di's younger son.

He turned to his brother: "Did you know Mom's a racist?"

"Go ahead and ask them what the sign says," she'd retorted.

At the same time, a xeroxed Polaroid of a black cat with red highlights had appeared on every telephone pole in the neighborhood. Lars was beloved and missing, and a typewritten paragraph described a larger pattern of cats being stolen off sidewalks for use as bait in dogfighting rings: Not in their neighborhood. Keep cats indoors. Report suspicious persons.

She could hardly open the car door against the Chinese people's fence, and she had to angle out as if she were the two sides of an arrow.

A boy-girl couple with tiny clothes, stylishly slept-in hair, and a hosiery of tattoos paused before the sign with the Chinese characters.

Suddenly she wished she hadn't wasted so much energy trying to fit in. It did her no good now to have been skinny long ago. Her brain was a chicken breast, her headache wrapped with cellophane.

The Chinese mother—there were teenage girls, or maybe they were in their twenties—came around the side with a rake and a bucket. Sonia had not even officially introduced herself. Just some apologetic little waves. Why apologetic? Why was it easier to love strangers? Just the other day, in the hushed, lunchtime line at the post office, everyone resigned to wait for an audience with the ageless witch with porcelain cheeks and horse-tail hair behind the counter, Sonia had been an emissary from Planet Smile. Behind her a young university dad wore a BabyBjörn, the straps crossed between his shoulder blades, and she smiled at the baby—Japanese dad, Japanese baby, Japanese address on the manila envelope in need of posting. She'd smiled at the Botoxed lady in beige wearing sculptural sunglasses; at the slabby hipster chasing green martians up stairs and around corners on his phone. What would the Japanese baby remember from his first few years? What overheated ice age was he headed for? Wasn't it the truth, as Ruth said, that Botox made white people look like aliens?

There was a weedy old shack-dweller with his back to the room filling out labels. Unwashed jeans, uncut gray hair. Suddenly he turned around and faced his flock: "Nobody talks to each other anymore! Unbelievable!"

Nobody looked at him.

"I was liking the silent camaraderie," said Sonia.

He pretended he didn't hear her and lurched toward the door, cutting through the line where she stood and tripping over her boxes. He had to put a hand on the dirty floor to catch himself. The Japanese dad bent instantly to right Sonia's boxes, and the baby, suddenly lying on his back in a hammock, stared up at his father.

The Chinese mother was inspecting the thorn tree that grew in the strip of grass between the street and the sidewalk. Its leaves were secondary to its thorns. In fact, thought Sonia, the whole tree must have been an accident, a weed that had escaped notice until it put wood on its bones.

The Chinese mother jerked her head at Sonia, and Sonia did her windshield-wiper wave. They were fifteen feet away from each other. Sonia could see her elbow fat, calves cinched by white socks, plastic shower sandals. A bruise like the Nike swoosh under one eye.

A bulletproof Escalade rolled slowly up Weymouth. Sonia heard the deep, dusky honks of a fire truck on the busy cross street at the bottom of the hill.

What does your sign say? she imagined herself saying. How would she demonstrate that she respected the mystery of the Chinese characters?

The sirens grew louder and wilder, and the hook and ladder rotated onto their street, got its footing, and hauled up behind the Escalade.

"Pull over!" cried Sonia. The hulking Escalade was oblivious. There was so much injustice, so many brave firemen and soldiers in the world! Her heart was pounding. The fire truck leaned into its horn now, and suddenly the SUV accelerated and roared off through the intersection.

"That makes me so mad!"

Sonia realized she was staring at her neighbor. The childlike nose. It wasn't negative. Asian women had beautiful skin, Black women had beautiful shoulders, and white women—not Sonia, unfortunately—had beautiful eyebrows. There was no deeper meaning.

"What does your sign say?" she asked before she could stop herself.

The Chinese mother rushed to lean her rake against the thorn tree. Then she stood perfectly still before Sonia except for her hands, which were thrown into a flying frenzy.

She didn't speak English. How was that possible? Right next door—how was she not living in terror?

Sonia climbed her wooden stairs and pushed open her front door. "Boys?" she called into the darkness. She whispered, "Princes?"

A SEDUCED WORLD

They were clearing a space for an artist demonstration, and I was jamming DVDs in the slot of shame. My kids thought that was hilarious, dogs in cones. I barely glanced at the plasticized covers. Had anybody fed them into the machine, sat patiently in front of the big old TV screen? Not to my knowledge. "You have a new memory," said my phone. A ripple from the abyssalpelagic zone—I looked it up—of zeros and ones.

Meanwhile I was still assimilating to the answering machine.

The librarians seemed like minor gods. Patient as stones. One in particular sat lost in a book, reflexively twirling the same lock of hair. She'd look up, startled, but still too young to be pained; it was her first job. Once, in line, I'd heard a pillar of the community say, "You're not from around here."

Lightly: "No, ma'am."

I liked that young librarian so much I loved her. I leaned across the counter when it was my turn with this tender satisfaction that comes naturally to me sometimes: "Her whole entire life," I said, looking after the busybody, "she's never been shut down." Of course I too wanted to know where our new girl was from.

I brushed past the sign for the artist now, seniors stutter-stepping on each other's arms, 3D Christmas-scene sweaters year round. A big no-nonsense minder with a pixie cut and a shapeless coat had her eye on them. I knew the going rate was seventeen dollars an hour. It was something women my age could do.

I was out the door but then, why not me? I turned around and took a folding chair at the back of the room. It was really something to sink down, even for just a moment, to lay my powers down.

The artist placed a shabby pine cone on the table like it was a whole tree. She fixed her eyes on the far wall as her hand moved on thermals, or along the planes of an imaginary Ouija board. The crowd gawked as if they were one single moron, and her speech sounded a little hypnotized: "Blind contour."

Finally, grandly, she lifted her drawing hand from the page. With practiced surprise, she encountered her work for the first time. Was she pleased? She held it high for all to see, and it looked like a record of damage, all missed circles and broken lines.

JANUS

Our first fall in Seattle, we were interesting. Being new, a new string of symbols, we were interesting because we were interested—being new. I wrote down all the nonsensical numericals, accounts and confirmation codes between me and the abyss, but for the first time ever, the landline had no reference to the land. We were invited to an election-night party by people so rich I related to them as gods. In their spheres luck was law and death did not deal. Of course death dealt. But money lived on. The wife was professionally beautiful, the rich guy was older, with older children, even grandchildren, and now this new brood of four, all runts, all looked like him.

We turned off the main road and gave our name at the guardhouse. It was the kind of deep-green November darkness that, having finished with the sky, moves on to the ground. It was the election that was supposed to change everything, you know the one I mean.

Odie asked to turn the light on so he could read. No, no, I hushed him. Moms in jodhpurs at pickup—we were passing the stables. Odie was humming "Here Comes the Bride." I'd left my wallet on top of a gas pump that morning and someone had attempted to buy a Nissan Pathfinder in Federal Way. Could I blame them? We made a final turn, and emerged in the cobblestone courtyard of a Tudor castle lording it over Puget Sound. Odie said, Is this a *house?* Mom! Why didn't you let me bring my sword?

It didn't take long to ascertain that we were the only guests who hadn't hosted a campaign-trail Barack in our living room. A couple of hale dads had just piloted their own planes out of Montana, a last-minute dip, vote-gathering. The moms were equestrians, ski queens, glass artists. I flattered my fears and prejudices, declaring myself against all equipment-rich activities. My son's sword was a stick; its superpower was that it looked like a stick but was really a sword.

The vibe was light patriotic, kids running a little wild. The theme was soul-food picnic, macaroni salad and collard greens. Please let the watermelon be well meaning, I thought, noticing at the same time that I was dressed the same as the help, a reliable narrator in a white button-down and last year's blue jeans. Well-meaning meaning another loophole for white people. There was a TV the size of the side of a truck that made state after state going for Obama seem like a Ralph Lauren ad.

*

Our house in Seattle had boarded seven nonrelated tenants before we moved in. Six tiny bedrooms plus the dining room, the only bath on the upstairs hall. Microsoft paid for our cross-country move, but the Three Stooges handled the packing. One box held half a little boy's sock drawer in a hornet's nest of paper, a fistful of second-string stuffed animals, my diaries from high school, and my husband's kitchen knives.

Every single window was freshly painted permanently closed. The front doorknob twisted off, releasing handfuls of hardware across the floor. The locksmith had a hatchet job of an accent and charged five hundred dollars to point me up the street to QFC for WD-40.

I shuffled up to my office. I had no work and nothing to say. Back downstairs. The kale in the fridge was springy, like hair, cabbage-y, from California. Not Washington State's clove-dark soil. The chard was from California too, the cilantro—and my thoughts tapered to a greasy-spoon vegetarian in the East Village, dishes with names like martial arts, everything topped with shaved carrots, the tang of the walk-in fridge, my roommate the ex-ballerina with her copper pots like Russian nesting dolls, her Williams Sonoma employee discount, stir-fry—Her beauty would have frozen Facebook. Google spat back her name.

*

I picked up the Burke-Gillman Trail at the end of Stone Way and walked along the canal that connects Lake Union to the Ballard Locks, and then to Puget Sound. I didn't understand how the fresh water and the salt water kept themselves straight, but I knew I wouldn't Google "brackish." I'd seen the salmon, toothy and haggard, jump the steps behind the glass wall at the interactive exhibit. They looked like alligators.

On the way back, I passed the Google cafeteria with Google-colored chairs and tables. It could have been a kindergarten. Over my head cars and trucks hammered the Fremont Bridge, hormone headache of the Fremont Troll.

*

I Googled an old friend and found her talking about her new novel and her old life. It was a phone interview, and her voice sounded like a translation, an oboe becomes a keyboard, but her laugh was the same. Frank and becoming. If only I could talk to her now, I thought, thank her for everything.

I listened eagerly, even greedily, but while my old friend sounded spontaneous, even careening and ebullient, she was actually practicing a strict code of discretion. To be honest, all those whose names she didn't mention would have liked feeling known. It wasn't my name I wanted to hear, but the sense of eavesdropping on my own past with someone else as the main character.

*

Each fifth grader was to choose a Greek or a Roman god. A contingent of cool boys, degrees of popularity according to their parents' origins at Microsoft, went for prominent warriors. One of those boy's fathers was a Harvard tight end, another was a porcine, peg-legged hipster whose startup had been acquired, allowing him to fund his wife's pursuit of the Dalai Lama. The cool boys had recently become horny, said my son. They were constantly asking him if he wanted to have sex—not with them, he clarified. He came home chanting lyrics from one of their favorite white rap groups: "No more Mr. Nice Guy, Imma take you home and fuck you twice guy." Odie chose Janus.

Janus, Roman god of beginnings and endings, of gates and doorways. Of January? I asked. November, said Odie. He was newly affected by the random. His back was perfectly straight at the kitchen counter. He slithered off the stool and assumed a matter-of-fact Vitruvian Man in the doorframe.

As the research progressed, it began to seem that Janus was the god of everything. Odie pointed out that this cheapened his power. Maybe diffused? I suggested. I wondered if Google was the real cheapener. Although it was undeniable that Janus was two headed as a common coin, with one site going so far as to say that since he had no Greek equivalent, the Romans gave him every attribute not already claimed by a Greek god.

Leftover powers. There was a template for the project, five sentences per paragraph and so on, and a box in which students were to drop a visual element. The whole thing went right into the portal, from which the teacher retrieved it, and I couldn't seem to let go of my distress about the zipless technology.

*

My laptop was still the family laptop, and it was always making the rounds. I didn't have the heart to find it in Odie's blankets now. Although surely what I was avoiding was making beds, gathering laundry. Anyway, there were skids of papers across my desk to last me all day. A traffic summons courtesy of King County—I'd run a red light, and to prove it, there were three color photos of the butt end of my car.

1. The old minivan, the spirit animal, poised at the head of the line in the left-turn lane. The trees on the median strip

were bare. A clutch of port-à-potties with belts around their middles waited to be retrieved.

2. The car's hips, the familiar profile, had completed the left turn through the intersection. The red light above was a bad moon.

3. A close-up of the license plate, which I always failed to memorize.

Did I really do that? Was the citation a record from the dream world? I couldn't figure out if waking life wreaked havoc on dream life, or vice versa. My dreams were repetitive, and episodic. Stuck in traffic down I-5. Stuck in traffic down Roosevelt. I gripped the wheel over the grates and grooves of the University Bridge, the double-layered I-5 bridge far above, a bicyclist sheared by, the boys in the back of my car were singing an a cappella tribute to John Williams one of them found on the Internet, until Odie executed a DJ-worthy transition to "Hallelujah" by Leonard Cohen. "Your faith was strong but you needed proof, you saw her bathing on the roof," was I dreaming?

I'd never been much of a connoisseur of information, even as a teenager I eschewed lyrics, life was moodier, more mysterious with mondegreens. How many times had I listened to Joni Mitchell's "Little Green" before I found out she was singing to the baby daughter she gave up for adoption?

In the rearview mirror, I watched the littlest boy in carpool pretending to read *The Lion, the Witch and the Wardrobe*, hoping one of the older boys, but not his brother, would notice. Just then Odie announced that it was blasphemy for Maisie in his class to point out all of his mistakes with the preface, "As a feminist . . .

What mistakes? said the other older, cleverer boy.

*

Then the laptop overheated in the blankets, and the battery swelled in its brain. There was an elaborate ritual over the phone, demanding a virtuosity of attention and fine motor skills, like playing the organ, with long silences during which I prayed.

*

A performance component had been added to the Janus project, and we pulled together a paper plate that gave Odie eyes on the back of his head—a two-faced mask. On the day of the presentations, I lingered at drop-off. I realized it must have been a year since I'd set foot in his classroom, when I'd chaperoned the field trip to the Nordic Heritage Museum. I noticed that many of the girls had grown fatter since then, like their mothers, and they reminded me of bar wenches in a Restoration drama—more contrived, less sensitive than they'd been in fourth grade. I slunk away, half heartbroken, as I always felt when I breached school during school hours. I got back in the car thinking about developmental stages. Even the little article I'd read the night before on the Internet about the cute opossum discovered on the subway, at my old stop, West Fourth Street, bragged about the life of the group opossum being five million years versus two short years for an individual marsupial.

Instead of going home I swung out to Discovery Park, five hundred acres of meadow, bluff, and beach wrested from the Duwamish, Suquamish, Tulalip, and Muckleshoot people before Microsoft. I crossed the fields at the top of the park and the oddly *Pleasantville* street with a row of military houses. One of Odie's classmates lived there; his mother was deployed and his father was a K-9 officer. The Olympics, unshrouded, were always stacked higher and more shining over Puget Sound.

I skirted the sand dunes. Stairs plunged down the sea cliff through nettle and salmonberry, ageless sword fern. I came out by old bunker bathrooms overgrown with blackberry and I could taste the smell of the water-treatment facility. I passed through a grove of freckled, tempered ash.

I stopped to watch a lone paddler off the northwest shore. He knelt on his board, using his bare hands as oars. The image seemed inviolable, but I briefly imagined writing a rescue scene. I'd have to engineer him falling in the water, requiring the kind of painstaking technical writing, brushwork, I always gave up on before I even began. And because the quality of those days—contrary to what I called them, the householder years—was an open doorway, a whoosh with no beginning, middle, or end, I felt I couldn't hold anything long enough to write it down.

When I got to the beach, the tide must have been record low. It seemed possible to walk barefoot all the way to Bainbridge Island. I took off my shoes and the mud had a latex, a skin. When I stepped on sea creatures they spouted. It was as if the tide had turned the water inside out. There was a word for that, evaginated. The floor burbled with geoducks as big as horse penises, barnacles hot in the uncanny white sun, and suddenly the mountains were everywhere, animated, as if they were finally set free.

MOTHER'S HELPER

My youngest, Bowie, was three. You could have put him on the city council, but I was still lactating. A picture in the paper of an Ecuadorian boy who had waded across the Rio Grande, planted pigeon toed now at the edge of his new schoolyard, backpack strapped on tight, tummy slack, and I would begin leaking.

Daniella was seven and Fin was twelve. I'd spread my children out so I wouldn't have to answer for my lack of heat, my failure to distinguish myself career-wise. I worked part time, from home, another hedge against the big contemporary questions. I'd been able to count on expressing a few drops in the shower for years.

We lived on College Hill in Providence, a historic grid heavy with trees. The Ginsbergs—the story begins—had arrived the fall I was newly pregnant with Bowie. They took it upon themselves to rescue a house hopelessly incompatible with the twenty-first century: eight thousand square feet of lacrosse-team slums, Suboxone dispensary, and most recently, tax write-off for a developer who defaulted before bringing it up to code, so that it was sold to the Ginsbergs minus heating and cooling, with all its best windows knocked out by lacrosse balls.

Lucia Ginsberg's daughter Anaklara and my Fin were in the same third-grade class. We often walked to school together, the six of us, that fall; I, a little seasick against a private undertow, and Lucia in narrow, tailored work skirts that caught her at the knee, chopping her stride. I can still see Daniella in the stroller, twisting around in excitement. But by October, Lucia had concluded that the neighborhood was safe enough to send Anaklara and her older brother Jerome alone, and if I was miffed to be cast as chaperone, I was also honest with myself about having forfeited some stature, and it was true that Lucia could count on me, so there was no use resenting the fact that I was part of her plan.

The lovely Anaklara, blended name from two grandmothers, an old soul of a girl with chipped fingernails and shoulder blades like broken wings, assumed an immediate and effortless intimacy. "Laurel!" she'd call out, running to catch up with us in her uncoordinated, almost nerveless style, as if she weren't quite sure whether it was her arms or her legs that should exert themselves. She'd grab my hand to pull herself the last few paces, while Jerome jogged behind, and I found myself feeling rewarded.

The males of the species talked wall ball, Jerome old enough to know he could toy with Fin, but making a point to abstain. Anaklara always had sweet words for Daniella, but it was to my adult intelligence that she was drawn.

In fact, even though she and Fin were the same age, I can't remember I ever thought of Anaklara as one of his friends, and although he would soon enter a boy-centric phase, a kind of developmental misogyny, in third grade he still respected girls. When I gave birth to Bowie (Beau a family name from when boys were suckled on sugar water, like hummingbirds) in June, Anaklara came to visit me in the hospital as she and I had planned, Lucia accompanying her, trying as best she could to tiptoe in her high heels. She stood awkwardly apart, flowers in a tight cone, while Anaklara knelt to peer at Bowie in the swaddle. "Look at him all nestled." Those hospital cottons, ergonomic cocoons.

I had the sense that Lucia was fighting the impulse to apologize for her presence—we both knew it was unearned—but at the same time, she didn't want to draw attention to the fact that her daughter's and my relationship not only took precedence, but might not, to us, seem strange. There was something complicated, too, unexpressed, about Anaklara as my initiate. But then Raffi came back from the vending machines and relieved Lucia of the bouquet, and in a neighborly way prompted her for details on the earthworks, feigning interest in the fact that the Ginsbergs were putting in all new trees.

"Did it really hurt?" Anaklara was asking me. "Ana K!" Lucia cried.

"No," I said truthfully, a lie.

I had always been told I was lucky to have easy babies, and my self-satisfied, albeit silent, rejoinder was that I was easy, easygoing, and made them that way. Still, when Anaklara asked shyly if she could be a mother's helper, I welcomed the chance for company and an extra pair of hands. She walked herself to our house in the mornings and home again after lunch when Daniella had her rest time. She had natural curiosity and abundant instinct, but what continued to surprise—and sustain—me was that all the while we talked like friends.

We seemed, in fact, secretly delighted by what the other had to say, and at lunchtime I found myself sitting down with a matching plate of food, and with a kind of attention for another human that I'd been defending against for years.

Fin barely noticed that I'd made such a friend. There was a new trampoline a block down, and he was part of the pack that cased it, circling closer, waiting for their turn. The few times that summer I ran into Lucia she was half sheepish and half proud of her dedicated daughter, whose praises I sung, although it wasn't that simple, and we both knew it, and told ourselves we had Anaklara's best interests in mind.

Only two or three of the Ginsbergs' new trees died. They must have come with some warranty. Ours was a neighborhood that accommodated life cycles. New families, like the Ginsbergs, replaced professor couples who seemed to shrink, shrivel inside the listing old houses over the years. But that summer in particular, our bedroom windows open, BioMed dirged, and it was hard in the middle of the night not to think of lab monkeys poking their bare hands through the bars.

Fourth grade started, with Fin and Anaklara in different homerooms. On our morning walks to school, now minus Jerome, who biked on his own, Fin would string himself out ahead of us so as not to be seen with her. Daniella started pre-K, and Bowie and I walked again to pick up his siblings every afternoon. When she saw us, Anaklara would rush to the head of the corral and push her arms through the chain-link to the elbow. "Laurel! Bowie!" Other kids looked askance; some stared. "You're going to get stuck," warned a teacher in a mocking tone.

Fin and Daniella would jostle their way through while Bowie, in the pouch, worked his new kickers like a rabbit.

"Can we take Anaklara home?" I asked once, and the teacher turned her wit on me while addressing the whole crowd: "No one escapes aftercare." Kids watched in awe and she added thrillingly, "Lock 'em up and throw away the key."

The following fall, Lucia—and Paul, I'm sure the Ginsbergs were feminist parents—switched Anaklara to another private school, and once a week or so I'd see petite Lucia in the cockpit of that enormous SUV, driving carpool.

There was a new wave of social-justice consciousness and people in our neighborhood were putting up yard signs. We had a middle-schooler, Fin was in sixth grade, and one night at dinner our firstborn looked out sideways from his shaggy boy-band bangs to say, "Hey. We should get one of those Black Lives Matter signs."

To be honest, Raffi and I both recoiled. Wasn't there something ostentatious, hypocritical—in the context of our nearly all-white neighborhood—I cast about for the right word. Or was it a kind of white flag—not that there was a race war. Of course Black lives mattered, but did Fin understand that the statement was actually negative? That the sign was reminding us that the matter of Black lives mattering wasn't settled? Raffi said to our son, "How about telling us what you think it means?"

I wish I could say here, out of the mouths of babes, but it was clear from the way Fin faltered that he had only identified a marker of cool. Later, in bed, two adults on their backs with the overhead light still on, Raffi said Fin had sort of called our bluff, and I said we'd never even had a bumper sticker, and we tried to laugh it off.

The poster tube arrived, and I unfunneled it as Daniella hovered lightly by my side. "Finny's sign," she said a low, reverent way. Bowie marched in place to mark the occasion, and Daniella melted away.

Bowie had discovered the little old bathroom under the eaves on the third floor, and he liked to pack himself in for a nice long poop up there. He still needed wiping, and one lengthening afternoon further into that temperate spring the doorbell rang just as I'd reached the top of the stairs.

"Don't answer it!" I called down, but I could already hear my older children running for the door. Stranger Danger was what they called it at school, but I'd been wary of preemptively instilling fear, and so of course we'd ended up without rules. I'm afraid I left Bowie stranded, his little bare bum pointed helpfully in the air.

"It's for you, Mom," said Fin, nonchalant, midstairs, having fought off Daniella to be the bearer of news. I rushed past without a word, as if I were acting out some drama, and then realized startlingly that my son had thoughts of his own now. I paused to look back at him where he leaned over the banister. He shook his hair into his eyes.

He'd left the front door open, but the woman—a Black woman, "fallen on door-to-door times," was the phrase that ushered itself into my mind—stood watchfully in the farthest corner of the porch from the door. She averted her eyes as I stepped out, and it came to me in a second wave of dismay that she could have read Black Lives Matter not just as a sign but a *sign* —an announcement of my guilt, which was true, absolutely true, but in a more abstract way. She could have even taken it as an invitation, or to mean I thought I owed her something, which was also true, but seemed as I faced her to be very much my own personal affair.

She was younger than I, bare hips squeezed up and out of her jeans, and I caught myself staring at stretch marks like fresh wounds.

"Hi," she said, and it disarranged the air. She moved toward me, then stopped at a spot that seemed both too close for comfort and too far away for normal exchange. "Let me tell you a little about myself."

She blew up her cheeks. Our rhythm was off. "Born and raised in Ohio," she began, and I tried to pose listening. She nodded and looked around, as if to appeal to the setting. "At this time living homeless."

Did I appear sympathetic? I should have risen to the occasion of host, a guest on my porch, but instead I felt distracted. And just then, as if to prove my inhospitality defensible, we both heard from inside, barely muted by a maze of walls, a magnificent set of roars. It had to be said that Bowie possessed deep lungs for a three-year-old. I felt the line wound tight in my chest slacken, tighten again as I pictured Bowie hog-tied by his pants around his ankles missing a step, falling head over heels down the canyon of stairs.

I was about to excuse myself, but our eyes caught and held. She said, "I'm looking to get signatures for Khiara Dowdy. You know her?"

The Black Lives Matter candidate. I did indeed. We'd said to each other, Raffi and I, that we'd certainly support her down the road, but what was she, all of twenty-four? "Sorry," I said, and as if she'd been expecting it, the woman cut in, her voice rising, "You ever been to Ohio?"

I heard my closed-down, "Sure."

But she was shaking her head, answering herself, "I bet you've been to somewhere nice like Cincinnati, looking at you, but you ever been to Columbus? Where I'm from?"

Without waiting for my answer, she pulled a beat-up vinyl album from her luggage, and a legal pad with a long list of signatures. Here came the moment I'd been dreading, that she would ask me for something, and I would withhold, and the fact that it was playing out exactly as I'd expected made me feel floaty and foretold. "These here your neighbors," she indicated down the pad. I looked at the names on the yellow page. My neighbors? Somebody's neighbors. I glanced up at her smugly, permitting myself to buy into my own innocence, feeling now almost giddy, self-justified.

"Sure," I said again.

"Anybody ever help you?" It hung in the air. I started to answer, but she held up her hand. "I stand here before you like you got a heart like most people. But you never did have somebody like me at your door, now did you." An accusation of chance, I thought defensively, but my heart beat fast. I understood that were I to answer, it would not be to the question she had asked.

"I wish you luck," I heard myself say.

"All the luck in the world, that's you."

I thought I heard footsteps, and I turned to see Fin paused inside the door. My face was hot and my legs felt hollow. But she was finished, and as she banged her rolling suitcase down the stairs, she called, "Now *this* is what I call a bad neighborhood!"

The insult stayed with me for days, shifting at last to shame, then fear. I told Raffi but he brushed me off. "She wasn't exactly forcing you to sign." I brought it up again and he laughed, "Forget it. I don't think you made an impression on her, Laurel."

I happened to notice a new rash of stickers on the light poles in the neighborhood, "Fragility Is Your Safe Space," and "Political Correctness Is Halal." I looked sideways at the sign in my front yard. It was an especially quiet midmorning when the doorbell rang again—or the ring was louder than usual—in any case, it caught me lost in work and completely off guard. I suppose I might have cowered, but I found myself pouring down the stairs, and catching a glimpse through the sidelights, I felt a surge of anger meant to mask fear. I tightened my hold on the mug I had in hand—I could sling hot tea—and opened the door.

"Oh!" I cried, utterly disoriented, as if I were just now opening my eyes. It was Lucia.

"I like your sign," she said with a small, dry smile.

What could I say? She pressed her lips together. I'd obviously incriminated myself.

"I've lost Anaklara," she said then. It was a school day, and I found myself once more confused. She raised her eyebrows very high to keep her face from crumbling as she managed, "Is she here?"

There was a strange, stirred silence between us. I looked over my shoulder as if to prove I wasn't hiding any fugitives. Finally, I said, "Will you let me know when you find her?"

Lucia flinched. I knew it sounded recriminatory, but to apologize on top of it all would have only made the breach more obvious.

I should have said I'd heard through another mother that Anaklara was having a hard time at the new school. "Not academically!" I'd cried. The other mother woke her phone in a reflex of surprise, and giving me a punctured look she replied, "She's just one of those kids who gets isolated."

A few days after Lucia's visit, Daniella and I were watering pansies on the porch when up the block came Anaklara, looking like a ghost of herself, looking for all the world like a spirit without a home. "Everyone was so worried!" I greeted her, holding out my arms to the street below. Dutifully she mounted the stairs.

She hung her head, and I was struck by her lack of development. In fact, diminishment. She was, at twelve, very much a little girl, and I could see that Daniella felt it too, because she stepped up boldly, as if to an equal, and said, "Hi, Anaklara. Do you want to play or draw?"

"I'm sorry for causing you to worry about me, Laurel."

"Oh, my goodness!" My heart seized. A child shouldn't have to apologize to a grown woman. My shame, all of a sudden, at having let our friendship falter was so acute that I felt the bodily impulse to drop at her feet, beg forgiveness.

I shepherded the girls through to the kitchen, smalltalking all the way.

"Play?" said Daniella, "or draw?" Anaklara gave the younger girl a one-sided smile. "Use your words," whispered Daniella to herself in frustration.

Bowie grabbed himself a blue marker for emphasis: "Draw me one two free cats, Dani-please!"

Anaklara was arranging her markers in a mandala on her page. "What are you building?" said Bowie, shifting gears, and with an interest almost like gratitude.

I realized I had missed her, and it made me feel shy. I receded to the second floor to check the laundry, or my work email, or Bowie's room for stashes of food—he'd lately been playing an intensely imagined game about squirrels. I didn't want to hover. So I told myself. I told myself I'd go down soon and offer a snack, and by then my children would have worked on her, relaxed her back to her natural grace and intelligence.

I was doing web design for a local arts initiative. As Raffi said, the organization was a henhouse, and as I sunk into my cubby office off the laundry room, I had dozens of busy, peckish emails. I allowed myself to be first distracted, then absorbed.

I lost track of time. I had, I reminded myself at one point, trained Anaklara as a mother's helper, and now she was old enough to babysit. The emails seemed to fill back in as soon as I cleared them, and an hour had passed when I finally came to. I froze, listening, but there was no answering commotion from downstairs. For a moment, I imagined the worst, and at the same time there was the low hum of guilt, living with children, that I had not given enough of myself, that they would have been raised on the shortcomings of love rather than its abundance.

I stopped to listen again at the top of the stairs, and there was Bowie, speaking in his squirrel voice from deep inside a kitchen cabinet as he sorted pasta and beans. I made my way down, and there was Daniella, still drawing, with a quality of concentration like scholarship, and—Anaklara's paper, I saw, was bare. "When did she go?" I said, a small panic rising once more, "Why didn't you get me?"

Daniella looked up from her work. "We didn't want to disturb you," she said, so naturally, so peacefully, that I told myself I'd done nothing wrong.

I should have said, once again—but memory is no timeline—that Bowie had begged and pleaded—begged and pleased, Daniella used to say—to go to school like his brother and sister that fall. There was a nursery classroom for three-year-olds, and the strong-willed social savant, the third child, had prevailed. The mornings were surprisingly short and hectic now, and I often had to jog to school to make the pick-up at noon. Bowie insisted on carrying a backpack, which was, he told me, "very filled with important collections," and Raffi thought the whole thing was a riot, which offended me, and so I comported myself, vis-à-vis Bowie, with utmost sobriety and care. The new schedule pushed the housework into the afternoon, and at the same time, Bowie expected great things from me, now, having been out in the world.

One morning, not long after I'd dropped all three children off and returned home again, I sensed a presence on the porch even before the small knock came. My neck hairs tickled, and I sidled quietly to see. I did a double take—until this moment I might have actually believed that children ceased to exist during the school hours. It was Anaklara.

"Hello there!"

"Your azalea is like a red dress," she said, stepping on her own toes.

"Look at that," I said. It was.

"I'm home sick today."

"You are?" I smiled.

"I'm allowed to," her voice rose.

"It's a good thing to take a break every once in a while." I led her into the kitchen. Behind me she said, "I hate school." I pretended not to hear. She elaborated, "The girls are boy crazy and the boys are crazy."

I had to laugh. At least it came naturally, and she took it as a sign to climb up onto a stool. I said, "Do you have a friend or two?"

There was a pent-up silence. Heat spread from her neck to her cheeks until it reached her eyes and she couldn't hold back tears. I swept around the island to hug her. "Oh, Anaklara! Let's sit down," and I drew her to me and walked her into the living room.

She folded up her insect legs and pressed herself against me. I held her close and I could feel her heart pound. I didn't know what to say, but after a while, she closed her eyes, and gradually, as I looked down, the lids stopped flickering. I thought she might have fallen asleep, and I wondered if I was going to get any work done at all, but at the same time, those emails seemed suddenly very trivial compared to the clarity of Anaklara's need to be here.

Her hand crept out from her body and found my bare stomach underneath my sweater. My skin jumped in surprise but words appeared, as if lit from within: oh creature, oh comfort. I saw us as if I were watching from across the room.

"Do you still have milk?" she whispered. I was taken aback, but what seemed most important was not to distress the quiet between us. And so, "Yes," I said, "I do." And I was flattered too, that she apparently found me easy to talk to, easy in my own body, natural.

"May I nurse, Laurel?"

I was shocked, but from far away. It took a moment to register. I wasn't really shocked. My breasts were tingling, and I was already letting down. I eased her across my lap. I pushed up my bra, one of those stretched-out old sports bras, easy to maneuver, and guided her to my nipple. I understood that she knew exactly what she needed. Who was I to deny her wisdom? She latched on effortlessly, getting to work with a delicate confidence. My foremilk flowed freely. She closed her eyes. Her short, dense eyelashes were curled.

I thought she dozed, after a while, with a kind of sweetness that was not quite innocence. My other breast became full, and it throbbed as if it had its own heart. It was leaking shamelessly. She woke, and without opening her eyes or saying a word, switched breasts, and I was a geyser.

I had a lump in my throat. The power of the release left me hollow. I thought of Lucia, and sweat broke out on my lower back where it was pushed into the sofa. My armpits. The suckling had scrambled my brain, I thought. But it was too late now.

I'm just now remembering that there was a neighborhood possum who recurred in our backyard for years. If we went away in the summer for a week or two, she would have spread out, let down her guard. We'd gather to watch her from upstairs. "What should we do?" we'd say. But the truth was we took it for granted that she would go back to being invisible once we'd reestablished ourselves at home. We all assumed she lived alone. She grazed like a cow. She skewed our sense of scale. Suddenly our little yard was a pasture, even a sweeping field.

GREAT CATHEDRALS

The gods had heads like stones. Stone by stone awoke, she woke, starting at the center of the sleeping earth and splitting—

spitting atoms. Gravel. Her mouth was dry. Stay away, awake, no, wait, I'm coming.

You know the drill, said Mr. Madrigal. She had to get to school. First period. English? What drill? Before the stones

caved in on her. Mr. Madrigal was all blond, like a lion. She'd seen a lion at the zoo and it was so small, half the size of the lion in her imagination, pacing the pen with a passionate claustrophobia.

He played basketball after school, he couldn't jump but he could crouch way down and chest-pass with this flinging. Feeling. Boys copied him, laughing. He went wild when they scored. Oh, wow. It was different this time, the eye inside her head was that smell. Her mother's vomit on her sweatshirt. She didn't have another. Any shirt. So what. Get up. A car started, the smell of gas, and she knew if she could get to the window the dark would be caving in to gray. I'm trying to give you a feel for scale, said Mr. Madrigal. That smell was orange juice. If the nucleus of an atom were an orange, then the first orbiting electron would be five dark blocks away. Her eyes were oranges. But wait, said someone, wasn't this supposed to be English? Just testing, said Mr. Madrigal. Yeah, Mad G, why you telling us science? It's all the same, he said sorrowfully, switching his tail.

The men of Aramark opened the doors around six forty five. They rode wild mowing spirals over the grass and pincered trash. Took a ton of smoke breaks. They yelled at each other across the lime-lined football field, waved to her and called her Sweetie, Early Bird, Orange Juice. The foreman was a great-grandpa. The early bus was at five thirty. Just chance she'd discovered it one morning. Total

chance she was on that corner where it stopped, five blocks from the new apartment. This apartment. She fell asleep again but the gray

was the shadow cast by stone lions she'd seen at the zoo. Her phone buzzed under her hand. The screen was gray but here came the black, oh, wow—

The black split her head and a new head was a stone spit

polished as the bathroom mirror, gray, a good sign. She met her eyes. She lost them.

Her hair wadded against the cut in the back she couldn't see. She hadn't seen her mother coming, her mother with the frying pan coming up behind her. Lights out. Black cast iron.

Her hands met under running water. Mr. Madrigal said they were going to be doing more writing than reading. Personal writing, he said with sudden intensity—Why're you all up on us like a pusher? protested someone. Personal? Christina Emerson had tits in the J-K-Ls. You're flippin freakin me, Mr. Madrigal, said Christina.

*

He slammed snooze, somehow okay to abuse the old clock radio, living on borrowed time. He didn't really have to follow through till Annie got back from the gym with coffee. Although he liked to get to school early. Stake out his classroom.

Annie landed on the edge of the bed like an insect. Electric tights tiny as tweezers, punctuated, pristine sneakers. It was funnier to call her an insectivore.

She gave him a complicated look.

"What?" He sounded exactly like his mother and she looked harmed. What did she see? The last of his blond hair blown across his blushing skull, his small, round nose made him appear unserious.

She nested their empty paper coffee cups before conveying them neatly to the trash in the kitchen.

It was still dark but the little girls from the downstairs apartment were already marching around in rain boots and fairy dresses when he came outside carrying his bike. Annie had discovered they went to a very private school. His public high school was the lowest performing in the district. The girls stared at him unforgivingly.

There was action in the garbage bins against the side of the building as he was putting on his helmet. Skunks and groundhog types getting off the night shift. Was there no place to hibernate in the city, or did that come later in the season? Last week of October—still warm, although things were getting sculptural.

Distant sirens weaving, heavy trucks from the curve on the interstate that bisected the city.

*

The bus shaped out of the gray. She must have missed the early bus because it was Nellie, the driver, and Nellie's assistant, whose job it was to climb down at every stop and make sure the kids got safely on board. They said, Hi hon! Haven't seen you here—She sat right behind them. Nellie's assistant turned around to hand her an orange juice.

They passed the little old man with homemade posters propped up against his little old car by the entrance to the hospital. "Preborn women's lives also matter," "Hillary kills preborn women."

*

He passed the daily demonstrator, old crusader in front of the hospital. His mother called him her failed abortion. It shocked him. She said, "You can't take a joke even when it's on me?" Blah blah blah, went his inner voice, drowning her out, his antimother.

The pro-lifer had a lawn chair. Anti-choice, Annie corrected him.

*

Her head opened up again—nothing between her eyes—

but she felt for a handful of toilet paper that was already in her hand, and when she pressed the cut the axe was still stuck to the hills. The hilt. Her mother swung the pan by the handle.

Between the words was the meaning. But that was a good explanation for why her head was in halves.

Kids had already gathered waiting for the doors to open. No one said a word. She sat down on the curb. Blackness. She smelled—

Orange juice—

Vomit or gasoline—

*

He carried his bike in through the cafeteria entrance. As if wheels on the ground were a threat to the social order of the factory. Tater tots, hash browns, hot potatoes. Locked it around a steam pipe near the end of the dead-end hallway where the janitors had their den. "Ken," said Aaron. "Long night? Early morning?" Giant untied shoes and navy slacks, a grown son at home with the mind of a four-year-old.

*

She went in with the others, drifted past the salt and starch smelling cafeteria, climbed the gray rubber stairs. Mr. Madrigal said stairs made atoms. Stars. He apologized that he used to be a science teacher. Imagine a garden of stars. Seeding

the universe. She was trying to keep all the stars in the blackness. Trying to keep it word by word in the way

he said with writing. Each word a wake. Awake—

*

He almost forgot he was asbestosed out of his own classroom. The whole south wing condemned after an extermination company cynically called Birds and Bees had found a relic roof of asbestos shingles under the real roof. Pigeon infestation.

He dipped into the main office to make sure Kanter's classroom was open before he climbed three flights of stairs. "Just checking," and sure enough Main Desk Mari had to scare up buildings and grounds, the lowlifes who worked for Aramark.

"What else can I do for you, Mr. Madrigal?" said Mari. Better get back to that blinking dashboard, Aaron suggested, pointing.

He passed the fork in the hallway to the south wing, rigged with caution tape like a crime scene. The chubby guard, one black boot backed up against the wall, was absorbed in his phone.

Aaron paused. The guard removed his boot from the wall and crossed his arms. He had a diamond earring. A spiny, bug-eyed girl stopped in her motorized wheelchair. "No congregating," the guard warned them.

Kanter was out on paternity leave. Aaron happened to know the poor man was extending his vacation by teaching summer school, a deal if ever there was one with the devil-thy-name-is-woman. The door was unlocked, the doorknob was oily. Aaron had the urge to wipe his hand on the wall but found a hardened tissue in his pocket.

That sealed-up smell of nowhere for the smell to go hit him. He felt for the switch and as the energy-saver lights responded in shuddering stages, he saw he wasn't the first one in the classroom. There was a girl in the middle of the room, her head on her folded arms on the desk, her sweatshirt hood pulled up and over her head, full turtle. He slowed, quietened his movements.

The clock was wrong with no discernible relativity to real time. The god of time would have to come around with a screwdriver and take the cover off. Aramark? Kanter had been some kind of a government engineer before he turned to teaching. Why? Aaron had asked with routine sarcasm, in the teachers' lounge, and Kanter had said, Young minds.

*

A motor between her ears, the smell of gas-vomit, a purring—

She heard the light lion come in. Now she could sleep like a
stone. He was watching.

*

He skirted the sleeping girl to check out the lab at the back of the
room, provisioned with swivel stools and running water. Game
board of the periodic table, boxes on open shelves were Cloud
Chambers, Drivers for Foucault's Pendulums, Celestial Spheres,
Rando Wires. Still glad he'd switched to English, if only because
it required less gear. He was a huge proponent of pencil and
paper. He had voiced as much in a faculty meeting, when they
were talking about the budget for technology, and the principal,
Rae Spanner, had relished admonishing him in public, "You're
on the wrong side of history on this one, Aaron." He should
have invoked the door-to-door knife-sharpener, a grown man
with a bowl cut and dyed eyebrows, traveling with the tools of
his trade. Aaron used to feel mean just watching him approach.
He knew his mother would heave herself from the pit of the
sofa, fall back, relaunch, invent ungainly cross-steps to answer
the door. He could still see her hanging onto the frame to keep
her balance and then forgetting when she closed the door in the
knife-sharpener's face to remove her fingers. Aaron! He came,
although he didn't come running. Eggplant knuckles, nails that

fell off after a few months revealing new ones that were too soft, fetal, fused with the flesh of her fingers.

He meant to address some languishing one-paragraph essays, but the sleeping girl cast a bit of a spell. There was an argument for waking her up, but imagining the choreography made him feel creepy. Himself creeping up behind her—he'd let her be. For one thing, he wasn't sure which one of several minor girls she was, all of them breathtakingly thin and tenty as immature pterodactyls.

He went to the windows. That recurrent neighborhood woman, striding around the track with a book in her hands.

One of his last lessons before he quit teaching middle-school science and reconfigured himself for high-school English had been on the arbitrary nature of time zones. Star-time when his mother whacked him on the side of the head for coming home late, coming home early.

"Who here knows what time it is in England?"

In the silence—no takers—he could hear the clock ticking. Some sixth graders were infants, and some were sexually active. "Who knows what time it is in California?

"Nobody?" His incredulity never impressed them.

He took in hand a poison-smelling, squeaky whiteboard marker. "Chronosphere," he said as he wrote Chronos. His handwriting was symbolic. He had severe early arthritis. He'd chosen a black but it was a green, the caps betrayed him. Green wasn't a strong color. "From the Greek for—anyone?"

School was part of the pent-up violence of common

sense—the same as his mother's violence. She brought the chopping block down on his hands, cutting board, common sense, the first available weapon. He had no right to his students' attention. He spaced up and out of his body. Would they notice? Scarecrow down below wearing signature Air Jordans. The shirt was to keep the straw inside him—I'm your straw man for all of knowledge, he'd tell them.

Whoever had done the swabbing down had missed Kanter's skiff-y handwriting on the whiteboard, distant sails tacking one way and then the other. *Specific quantum transitions, spectralscopic parallax. Evidence.* Aaron stared at the terms.

He rose, thinking he'd erase the remnants of the astronomy lesson, but there was no eraser. His sleeve. He stopped himself. The temperature and composition of stars—people wanted to know—they wanted to know the truth—but all they could do was make up stories.

He took his sleeve to the whiteboard, wiping out the one hundred billion stars in the Milky Way. It would take three thousand two hundred years to count to one hundred billion.

One hundred billion neurons in our brains, one hundred billion atoms in a neuron. He loved the symmetry in science that made it seem like it came from a Source. Truth. Atomos, from the Greek. Meaning uncuttable. He'd wait a beat and then say, "Atomos? Anyone?" Supposed to make them laugh because of course he'd just given it to them. A meta trick. A positive formulation of a trick question.

He could use another cup of coffee. He could bring one back for the sleeping girl. But what if she came to while he was off chatting and this peace was ruined? He stared at a poster of the Great Cathedrals of Europe. Had Kanter selected it? What was it doing in a science classroom? At the end of physics was God. He took pleasure in giving Kanter a thumbs-up when they passed in the teeming hall between classes, Young minds, he'd say sweetly.

When the first buzzer sounded he nearly exploded out of his chair. To make up for being caught off guard, he stormed the door, glared down the hall to witness them amassing. Bare books in perennially bare arms; after a bomb threat they were no longer allowed the cover of their backpacks. Jostling, jogging, tagging, tackling one another. And laughing. They were always laughing. He retreated to his desk. The sleeping girl's feet remained planted. She was impervious as students filled in around her.

No outsize troublemakers in this section. "Christina," he called, as they were settling. "Go ahead and wake up your friend, here." There were three Christinas.

"Ooh, Mr. Madrigal," a chorister countered from the middle of the room, "Christina ain't no friend of June Poitras!" A tall girl, a six-footer with a huge front, lunged at the girl who'd spoken. Presumably one of the Christinas.

"Catfight!" cheered someone, echoed someone else—Aaron wasn't one those teachers who bore the mark, but he couldn't count on his authority. Couldn't count on being granted mercy.

"June stole Christina's *boyfriend*," a taunt rose above the others. Those weren't their real words—stole, and boyfriend—proper English was code-switching, he'd learned in a training.

"June and Christina's boyfriends," said someone, meaning girlfriends, lovers, and there was a flare-up of boys fist-bumping. Anything lesbian. Christina strutted in place, giving them her back, her broad shoulders.

It was impossible that the sleeping girl—June—was still sleeping, but Aaron didn't blame her for laying low. None of the kids seemed to want to get too close to her, and he had to wonder if there'd been a spectacular event, some extrajudicial upset of power. Look at her. A rag doll.

Aaron hit an imaginary timer with his flat palm. "Okay." Not that they had any reference for a real timer. He could feel his anger itch, suddenly. Just a little. Respect, apparently a relic, reality a game—but as he glanced at the sleeping girl again he could tell there was something off about the gravity. Those high-top sneakers with the heel built in—all the girls were wearing them. Wasn't it embarrassing? Her legs and feet seemed weirdly unfixed, marionetted to the floor. Indeed she seemed to be making the other kids genuinely uneasy.

He sauntered down the aisle between the desks to stand in front of her. There was no doubt in his mind now that he wanted to bring her to heel. To make an example of her shameless slumber. He pulled up a chair. The classroom went quiet.

But then someone tipped a chair, and someone mounted a desk to see better, and it didn't take a moment for Aaron's little spectacle to signal a free-for-all, all bets off, field day—man down. That was him. On his ass. The chairs were somehow three-quarter-size. He'd been sure June would wake up being watched, being breathed on, the way he was watching her, but her thick black sweatshirt seemed to absorb his stare. His mother would wake up if he stood in her doorway. Moaning, her hands already palpating her migraine, she'd work herself upright as he waited.

He placed his hand on the middle of June's back and the classroom volume crashed to near silence. A teacher couldn't touch a student. He waited, counting, breathing through his hand. No motion. His mother broke his hands because she could say it was basketball. But his hand was an instrument now, a Geiger counter. Was June radiant?

Who was that at his elbow? Theron, good enough. "Theron," he said, "Why don't you go get Principal Spanner." It was out of the question that he would leave the girl's side.

"Hi class, hello sophomores," he heard Spanner from the doorway.

"Mr. Madrigal's in the zone," said someone, to scattered laughter.

"Okay, let's check the drama," Spanner was saying, even as tall Christina called out, "We have a right to know what's going on, Ma'am!"

"You do not have that right, my friend," said Spanner, but bold Christina cut her off, "You are providing me a hostile environment!"

He wanted to laugh with them. He had no idea what was protocol, procedure. He felt that he was on the kids' side. To that end, without taking his hand off June's back, he said, "Principal Spanner. Thanks for coming by." She wheeled on him. What had he expected? He was no angel.

UNCOLLECTED TERRITORIES

My daughter, Mosie, called me early to remind me about the dentist. She was feeding the dogs, and I could hear them whimper and moan as she gratified them. The old dentist had suddenly stopped taking my insurance. I stood watching the lake, its blind surface—here I was, a condo with a view, but despite living my whole life in Seattle I'd never had any feelings for Lake Washington.

She had nothing else to say to me. Both of my children—Mosie and Basho—were first-time souls for whom the emotional was alien.

I could walk from the condo to the yarn shop, or Planet Fitness, and now, at the corner, I saw the bus already swinging low on the bus stop and I broke into a run. Woe was me, a hardy but unathletic child. Just as I arrived, the bus sank to the curb. I knew it didn't kneel for me, but I let myself feel flattered. Ahead of me, a great pile of human drove himself on board.

Hey guy, said the bus driver.

I'd shake your hand but I just took a shit. The voice from the wheelchair was almost buried.

The bus driver, on his own throne, said evenly, I appreciate your approach, Mr. Griffith.

I took a seat up front. It was impossible not to feel soiled. The bus driver pulled out of a heavy turn, straining against his harness.

I heard Mr. Griffith grunt, and I turned around. A runaway under a scaly blanket met my eye and gave me the finger. I'd brought my knitting in a Greenpeace bag, and I squeezed the challah of yarn. When Mosie was in seventh grade she'd become attached to a girl like that, a would-be juvie who cut her hair with a blade pried out of a lady razor. I'd overheard Mosie indoctrinating Basho, You know my friend Regina Spivak? She has *crippling* depression. Basho was making faces at his reflection in the turned-off TV screen, and I materialized in the doorway.

Crippling, eh? The skin around Mosie's eyes got red and punched-in looking. It wasn't usually so easy to destroy her.

How I had hoped, at first, that Regina Spivak would confide in me. There was something wonderfully subversive about bringing yourself down to their level. I'd gone so far as to picture myself invited onto the short couch in the middle-school principal's office. The currency in the girl groups Mosie was cut off from was emotional intensity regarding trees and whales, and I would ask the principal what he, personally, was doing about the environment. Being in his presence made me want to rake him over the coals, and confess my own anxieties about everything.

The bus window was abraded and greased, so that the sunlight seemed opaque, sourceless. I adjusted the knitting baby on my lap. I was guilty of canceling the Greenpeace membership after receiving the free tote bag. Someone pulled the cord for a stop, and the pressure changed as if the bus were trying to slow against its own strength on the runway. The runaway stalked up the aisle. Capitalist mutants! she shouted back into the bus as she descended. The bus driver closed the hatch, and it was as if she were sealed out—I looked for some sign from him that he'd done it to protect us.

Undoubtedly it was Regina who initiated Mosie to Tampax. I'd found the toxic shock syndrome warning unfolded on top of her bureau, and I snatched it up thinking I'd use it as proof—of what? That there was blood on her hands, just being a daughter?

She was eating cereal on our fat chenille sofa. Why are you using a fork? I demanded. She raised the offending utensil to show me how she was chasing Os up each tine, how it could take all morning.

The brakes let out a sigh, and the bus rocked from side to side before moving forward. I was always late, as a personality, even a demographic, as if I were determined to fulfill the stereotype of the single mother. But this morning I'd allowed a full hour to get downtown to the dentist. Neurons that fire together, wire together, and hup! I'd told myself: this was the new, condo Sheila. I didn't even need a house key. There were touch pads, and I used Mosie's birth date for everything. My firstborn had come out powerfully knotted inward, a rock grown into roots, a contusion. They couldn't do the pushing for me, honey, and they sure as heck couldn't get in there if I kept on fighting like a marlin. The doctor must have been a billfisher. The same extraterrestrial white lights in the delivery room as at the dentist. As a girl, I'd thought the dentist was going to suck me out by the breath when I closed my lips around the evacuator.

I have no understanding of your fear of the dentist, Sheila, Mosie had stated on the phone this morning. That was how she talked.

I just don't like going like a lamb to the slaughter, I'd protested. A mutton, I added.

She doesn't like anyone telling her what to do, said Mosie, to the crowd.

I said, You know they can't even prove flossing. Silence. You do floss, Mosie. I felt my chest tighten.

Now I looked out the bus window without seeing. I'd learned limbic system breathing at a workshop. I felt my waters flush, a wave machine, until I remembered that the limbic system was more like rock formations. But I kept coming back to how I'd be forced to start from scratch, a whole new portfolio of medical history questionnaires and X-rays, glassy films of the teeth in my skull with their gristle of roots, sunless shadows. I imagined all those disclosures releasing their mists, their metallic aftertastes into the air and the water—

Take a Xanax, said Mosie.

I brayed, Pharmaceuticals are turning waterways fluorescent!

I could hear the dogs barking in the background. What's that about?

Cookies, said Mosie. Her husband said the dogs' libido was hunger. The barking got louder and I pictured her turning the phone into the yard for my benefit. The bus braked a full block before the traffic lights, and again it was like a pressure change at altitude. The air made painful caves in my ears.

It was a recent move for me, to Lake Forest Park, and I wasn't sure of the new distances up here at the neck of Lake

Washington. My ancestors were from the prairie. Starched grass, ghost choir. My mother, Maureen, was born in a dooryard packed hard and polished smooth as Mexican tile. Inside the house the menfolk were not to be disturbed. Wisps of cottonwood fleece, spackled sunshine, the woman at first doubled over and then drawn and quartered; then making her way on all fours to the shade side of the house, out of sight of the door and the single window. Between contractions she carefully removed her undergarments. She folded them and put them under a flat rock. She was forty-two years old, and Maureen was her first child.

I don't understand, I used to say darkly, why she couldn't tell the men she was having a baby.

Maureen said levelly, She washed me at the pump, threw the placenta to the pigs, and went inside to make dinner.

I never wanted my mother to go back in time to her mother. I'm not like her at all, I said stubbornly.

If protofeminism was timeless, strong and silent, I'd aged into a good witch look, in my big hats and coarse linen. Flax. I had never been to the prairie. Mosie took the hem of a tunic between her fingers. Mortification of the flesh, Sheila? My legs had not seen the sun in years, and unsheathed, they looked like they were defrosting. When I got up to the mirror I saw that my face had been balled in someone's fist and then released— it uncrinkled slowly. My mother stared back at me. What a cliché for a woman my age to become her mother, but the woman in the mirror was not Maureen at a correspondingly still-soft-eyed midfifties. I looked like my mother the night she crawled all the way across the plastic floor of her shared room at Shoreview, bloodless as an opossum, looking for death, and finding it when she reached the door they cruelly left open to the low-ceilinged, fluorescent-singing corridor.

They told me she expired at the threshold, and I cried, She was an outdoorswoman!

Is that right? said the administrator over her reading glasses.

The short-haired young mother across the aisle switched into her native Russian on the phone and suddenly started stroking her little daughter with great feeling. She caught me looking at her as a fellow single mother, and my eyes dropped in shame and glory.

Some mornings I lay on my back in my bed till noon, long divorced, still single, still, if truth be painfully told, living on alimony, releasing secret after secret. I didn't bother to open the curtains; Lake Washington would still be there. Strands of light off the water unraveled and danced across the ceiling, and I imagined all the essential, ancient people who believed in fate and god-systems were really talking about genetics. How cavalier I'd been in choosing the human yarn with which to weave my children. Chris Sheen. I'd had to keep my maiden name so as not to be Sheila Sheen, daytime starlet. I'd gone back to work after he left me, after being the Microsoft wife in clover. It was a startup to do with corporate self-discovery, subcontracting with the Myers-Briggs people, Enneagrams, What Color Was Your Company's Parachute? There was no proper HR department, so I was everything to everybody. And if I was going to smuggle Basho and Mosie past my boss when they had daycare daze, not to mention childhood diseases, I'd be obliged to parade my bready legs in miniskirts. As if it were good manners to demonstrate an openness to sleeping with him. I trained them to chirp, Thanks so much for having us,

Mr. Newcomb, but Mosie was all of five when she challenged me, Is Mr. Newcomb your boyfriend?

How else was I going to get a week off to visit my sister, Nina, when she had her first baby? She was older than me by a decade. Despite the fact that I slept on a cot in the basement and folded her laundry, I could finally lord it over her. My niece's name was Meridel, and her appendages were crooked and mottled, her bottom fleshy and without muscle. I couldn't read her eyes. It made me nervous when the cat watched her from a hardbacked chair, testing the waters with its tail, but I shared the animal's suspicion, as if the baby were a changeling.

For the first time, I missed my own children. Their voices sounded computerized, on the phone, and I could tell they didn't believe my voice either. My mother tried her best to report, but of course she didn't know them as I knew them. At last, I was banging my rolly up the front stairs of our little stucco three-bedroom, stiff rosemary bushes covered with delphinium-blue flowers, and I was struck by the feeling that I could see myself as Basho and Mosie saw me. The prodigal mother. I opened the door as if it were a precious thing to handle and peered down the dark hallway. Then the spell of my absence broke and I rushed toward them.

Basho, up until now my angel, redeemer after Mosie, never anxious, always vivid, took a firm step behind my mother. Mosie stood her ground, but I did not go to her. Basho! I pried him out and knelt to hold him. He was wooden. I tried to pick him up, but he made himself heavy, and I had to drag him across the room and onto my lap on the sofa. My mother's helpless look, as witness—

I pressed him crosswise to my breast in the old nursing position. Did he even remember? Mosie stood by, coolly observing, keeping her thoughts to herself as always. Tell your mother what we did this morning, Mosie, exclaimed my mother. She mouthed at me, *Listen.*

We saw our dad and our stepmother, said Mosie. My mother drew back sharply. Mosie circled her comfort hand through her hair. She liked how it felt between her fingers.

We did not, said my mother, sounding almost hurt, bewildered. We didn't at all, Mosie.

You never let me see them! cried Mosie.

My mother made a motion at me, but I matched my daughter, They don't want to see you, you ignorant child!

Out the bus window—where were we? The usual route was 522 on the diagonal to join with I-5, the main river, but we were dribbling through the neighborhoods. A pulse of yellow caught my eye. Mosie had desert-blooming Scotch broom in her dog-patch in Shoreline. A thrushy, overripe smell filled the air. The hounds were in heat, there was something pro-life, evangelical about it.

I could still sense the lake on the left, a quiet, cold contour. I used to imagine it started at the moon and flowed all the way down to Mount Rainier. But I never worshipped it. Something small and light dropped out of my hair. A translucent green worm, more plant than animal, took up where it left off and shrugged its way across my knitting. Mosie would have destroyed it immediately. Where had she come from?

Basho was a programmer; he worked for a game company. He practiced extreme solo sports, eschewed human contact, had dull eyes that I had seen star-shower like an IMAX when he sat before his computer. Every once in a while, he jumped out of airplanes. He was gay in an antifamily, antifuture kind of way. I kept this to myself. I had never met a boyfriend. I once asked Mosie if she had.

You've never been that close with Basho.

Stung, I countered, How does your husband feel about having a gay brother?

All guys have a little gay in them these days, said Mosie.

Mosie, only sixteen months older—I'd taken clomiphene— went by Maureen now, her birth name. She had married her first and only friend—Regina having faded—a ghoul in com- bat boots with a heavy blond forelock who was in eighth grade when she was a sophomore. He nuzzled her in my presence. How quickly I realized that Mosie hanging out with this Teu- tonic, six-foot-tall middle-schooler was worse than her being a short, fat Stevie Nicks, if Stevie Nicks wore a trench coat like a female school shooter.

I had hardly seen his eyes until the wedding, when he gave himself some kind of a warrior haircut, and then, of course, they were the eyes of the warrior's beast, huge, liq- uid, ready at any moment to be offended on behalf of the warrior.

When I was showing off for people, I called him by his last name, Straub, as if I were making fun of his masculinity. Mosie called him Stuber. His name was Stewart, which Basho annunciated in halves like *lose-er*.

The first time Stuber called me Mother Sheila I cried out in fear, and he looked on keenly. He shot me emails once a week headed Factoid. He never mentioned the correspon- dence when we saw each other. The oldest living human was born closer to the signing of the Constitution than to today, Mosie's husband wrote me.

When the bus dilated for a local stop, I could still smell Lake Washington. I wondered if I should start worrying about being late. A sisterhood of little dolls in glossy ringlets and masks of makeup fancy-footworked down the aisle. No one betrayed interest. Their chaperone brought up the rear—she had dead hair as if the girls had sucked the life out of her. She leaned into my seat to answer my look: Irish step dancers.

Mosie's beast managed parking lots. Now he looked like a skinhead, rolled in ink, cruising around Seattle behind custom tinted windows while Mosie watched his website, transported dogs in crates in her abused minivan. Mosie had told me herself that he was turned on by his own success, unforgiving in his dealings. How could I imagine he was forgiving with Mosie?

He said they weren't going to have children. Is that okay with you? I once asked her. She shrugged. I used to complain to my mother that Basho and Mosie were all vanity and no ambition. As babies, they could have saved the world. But they punted their childhoods. By the time Mosie was five, she'd slammed the book on storybooks, at seven she retreated from soccer—with her sturdy little body, she was good on defense—at nine she hated music, and she ended up squeezing through the only door she'd accidentally, it seemed to me, left open by the time she finished high school. Marriage.

But then again, why didn't I save the whales myself, instead of blaming my daughter for eating junk food in her minivan, leaving the wrappers?

We seemed to be on a latitude with Magnuson Park, which bulged out into the lake before tapering to the Cut, freshwater met salt, and university crew boats hauled from one pool to the other. The bus knelt again, and Mr. Griffith wheeled himself off capably. You have a good one, now, said the driver.

A handful of passengers watched and waited on the sidewalk. One by one they filed past those of us who practically lived on this bus by now, and we passed our silent judgment.

It was stop and go—I was sure it wasn't supposed to be a local. I was anxious again, and again I misimagined the limbic system. But water, water everywhere—Seattle was just an entertaining obstacle course for water.

The bus driver seemed to have a force field around him, and if he heard my cough of conversational initiation, he gave no indication. I wouldn't bother my knitting. In any case, I needed the time to frame the action. I needed to decide if I was controlled or exposed. Would I allow X-rays? I used to refer to email as Emily. Basho had regarded me with open horror. Mosie just laughed. Do you have a name for your indoor plumbing? I'd never been to the prairie, but I had authority problems going back to my grandmother's refusal to tell the men inside the house she was in labor. If I capitulated at the dentist, gave them what they wanted—

Recently, grudgingly, Mosie had agreed to drive me to the vast cemetery in North Seattle where my mother was buried. Empty dog crates slid across the hull of the minivan, banging into the bare metal walls at startling intervals, but I reminded myself to be on my best behavior. I told her I could smell the wet cedar tree beside my mother's stone, and she flipped off a driver who accidentally met her eye as he passed us.

The light was loose in the clouds, and I realized with some shock that it was late June, the sun playing hooky at bedtime, the time when schoolchildren were about to explode from educational bunkers across Seattle. I used to imagine they'd been beating on the doors all winter. The way they spun around and shot-put their backpacks at the kneecaps of their caregivers, swelled the neighborhoods, broke down doors, laid waste, set fire—by dinnertime of the first day of summer, they would have shrunk their parents down to tiny custodians.

What was I supposed to do with Basho and Mosie? Be my real self? Hand myself over, do what you will with me, plant your strange selves in my private soil?

Mosie said she'd wait for me in the car in the cemetery parking lot—she had tree allergies. You never had them on my watch, Mosie. I was aware that I couldn't stop worrying her like a dog with a bone, the rawhide twists she bought in bulk from Amazon. She made herself comfortable in her seat and picked up her phone from the console.

I don't even remember where her stone is, I said in defeat as I dismounted.

The woman behind the desk was a triathlete, but her face was completely ruined, so that she looked like a crone in a stolen body. She offered me coffee from a pod, creamer inside a tiny aseptic cupcake. The man leaned over the counter to make some lines and circles in rollerball on a foldout map I could take with me. I had already turned to go when for some reason I stopped and hissed, You know she's not really *here*, don't you?

I'd scattered my portion of Maureen's ashes at a retreat center that backed up on a broad creek in a grassy valley. My plan was to be there when the world apocalypsed and we had to share food and guard water. I had work-studied in the kitchen, so I knew there was peanut butter and chocolate and frozen soy margarine to last till we discovered life on Mars and dusted off our old prairie schooners. Passing the talking stick around the circle dignified loneliness, not so different, it occurred to me, from the way dignified men must visit prostitutes. I was a Pisces. My dreams were loaded with augury during my bleeding. Would my dreams dry up when I completed menopause? Powerful, Sheila, said the workshop leader.

I cast one last look at the minivan as I set out into the cemetery. Mosie could have used the exercise. Never would I have denied my own mother—and then I realized my tears were packed so tight in my chest it hurt, like breaking rock, to release them. How I missed her! I forged the grounds without heeding the directions.

There was a woman ahead of me on the road, plodding steadily beneath an enormous rain poncho. My prehistoric heart, thundering, couldn't help but recognize my mother.

I slowed to quiet my pulse. And to suspend the dream—was there any harm in it? I thought suddenly of a hiking trip in the North Cascades when I was just out of college and my red hair still had all its pigment. My mother and I in first-generation polypropylene tights, gathering mountain-goat wool from the prickle bushes. I let her take the lead. I didn't like the sense of having her behind me, of leaving her behind. Even then. Even when she was heavy and strong, her thick hair pulled off her broad forehead by mirrored sunglasses.

Traffic through Ravenna. So at least we were inland from Lake Washington. Outland toward Puget Sound—was it a real factoid that both the human body and Planet Earth were two-thirds water? You could almost say the same for Seattle. The couple behind me were grousing that the alternate route, which the driver was contractually bound to follow, had clearly been computer-generated in Bangalore.

It's not the usual route? I ventured, rubbernecking around behind me.

No, said the man flatly, speaking for both of them. Nothing further. I retracted. I wondered if the bus driver had heard me. I sunk my hands in my knitting.

Mosie and Stuber had a cookout wedding. She identified, she said, with his family. One of Stuber's cousins went online to become a Universal Life minister; he wore a T-shirt laminated with the front of a tuxedo. We all gathered under one of the BBQ shelters in Carkeek Park. We have a hitchuation here, people! said the cousin. Maureen and I were stuck at the back of crowd, second class citizens, like women and children.

Another cousin was pouring beer out of cans into plastic cups under the tablecloth. I would have declined, had I been offered. I approached my counterparts, Mosie's in-laws, who sat as one shelf of flesh, who had themselves been married beneath a picnic shelter. Stuber's mother reached over her husband's lap to clutch at me. Welcome to the family, Shirley. Did you see their cute tats? She held out her own ring finger, which was bare. I, in contrast, had always been good with names.

Mosie was busy talking to the minister as I picked up her chubby little hand and held it in mine. I wanted her undivided attention, but had I ever given her mine? Freely? I examined the wedding ring tattoo, its 3D gemstone. I checked to see that it went all the way around. Ouch, I said quietly.

There were burger buns in bags as big as bed pillows. Industrial-strength ketchup. Frozen pucks of patties—Stuber sidled up to me and said the two tattoos had only cost a buck fifty.

Chris, my ex-husband, made his way over to where I was stationed beside Maureen under a pile of coats in her wheelchair. Behind him was Riley, the creature-woman he'd left me for when the children were practically still in diapers. She's so sweet, whispered Riley, cocking her long head at my sleeping mother.

Quite the event, said Chris. Was it possible he had regrets? Would he have liked, finally, to walk his daughter down the aisle? All the fight had gone out of me. I felt that my memories made a map, but I didn't know how to read it.

Riley offered to stay by Maureen while I went to the beach to join the party. She pulled out her phone and disappeared seamlessly. Chris pivoted toward the daylight outside the shelter and turned into a phone also.

I crossed the grass and the parking lot to the pedestrian bridge over the railroad tracks that cut off the coastline. I paused at the top of the stairs, in the batting cage, to look out toward the Olympics. The mountains, as usual, had wrapped their statues with cloud burlap. Puget Sound was narrow here, as if Carkeek were a stop along a corridor. A wind came up, and the concrete floor seemed to be quaking. I looked down, and there was a gleaming oyster of bird shit.

Mosie on the beach, in jeans—At least white ones? I'd pleaded—and her new father-in-law's huge Seahawks sweatshirt. She was talking and laughing with her tribe. Stuber had shaved the sides of his head clean and spiked his forelock for the party. A cast of little kids screeched to the water's edge, then, arrested by a new idea, started throwing rocks at the white wedges that were seagulls.

I had no place there—raucous laughter, cold, metallic water. I could almost taste the treatment plant; there were shell-fish warnings everywhere. I pressed myself against the chain-link cage to see better. The cousins all seemed to have the same girlfriend, in cheap flared jeans and big hooded sweatshirts, and they all looked like my Mosie. I thought suddenly that I hadn't recognized her when she was born, either. She wasn't uglier than any other baby. She certainly wasn't more beautiful. But there was no answering chord. I named her after my mother in an attempt to naturalize her, domesticate her to me—replicate something of what I had with my first Maureen, my mother.

The couple behind me on the bus had begun arguing loudly. You're constantly bragging about how much money you have, and then have you noticed how everybody lets you pay for everything?

The man kept blowing his nose like a kazoo. Can't you ever let your mother pay for anything? The bus pulled over, and the broken couple disembarked. I leaned forward and gave the driver the dentist's address and asked if I should get out with them. He said I should wait for University. I thanked him as a form of apology.

I thought of a day my mother and I had taken the children for a hike up a small mountain above the flower farms and the oyster beds of Skagit Valley, north of Carkeek Park along the same water. Basho had to be lured with M&Ms; Hup, Bash, my mother kept saying, but Mosie was a born trudger. We made a big to-do about being on a leg of the Pacific Crest Trail, then we got off on a horse path and ended up at a small pond recessed in the forest. Gross, said Mosie, in her element. It was a congee of algae and frog eggs, islands of swamp-tuft connected by drowned trees made irresistible bridges. I ate the rest of the M&Ms myself, sitting on a log with my mother, watching Basho and Mosie, who were almost willing to be convinced by the water. It must have been soon after Chris left, and I remembered thinking that now I myself could go back to being a child.

The bus window was like an old sheet of plastic. On a recent flight out to visit Nina—Niece Meridel was off to college—my seatmate had talked about ducks getting caught in the propellers, feather pillows. Or maybe Rainier was shedding its weather, I suggested, webs of snow that had been woven all winter around the mountain. He looked at me blankly. When we cleared the Cascades, the earth looked like another planet. Inhospitable fissures, drastic temperatures—no life, no water. I felt disoriented. Had the moon been privatized? Was the project on Mars actually taking signups? Could you buy a Tesla at a Toyota-Hyundai dealership? I was sliding backward and forward indiscriminately. There were no special brakes, nothing to hold me in middle age. I felt I could see my death from up there; my seatmate offered me a drink with more concern than chivalry. Mosie didn't drink, so I had stopped drinking.

Maureen's mother, my grandmother, was from a time when it still wasn't clear if humans were going to be able to dominate nature. She lived on the prairie when tracts of grassland were unclaimed, at least by white people. And now my mind was the seat of self-consciousness re coal, nuclear, frack-ing. Greenpeace. The age of guilt. Great barges of melting ice, polar bears washing up on tropical beaches, their jaws impos-sible to open. I had no real duties. No plants, no animals. No survival issues. A one-bedroom condo with a balcony off the bedroom that looked through fernlike conifers to Lake Wash-ington. Buckled in, seatback and tray table and duck-hunting seatmate, I thought we were doomed. I couldn't imagine good old God as an environmentalist. How I wanted to go back to a time when the world had seemed to carry its own weight! When it could retain its own ice caps!

The dentist's waiting room was large and airy, on the fourteenth floor of a landmark downtown building. Framed photographs on the wall were for sale—muscular waterfalls, de rigueur Rainier, a steep-bank beach oppressed by drip-ping evergreens. I had arrived in plenty of time, but perhaps I should have heeded Mosie and got hold of some kind of pill—anxiety was the word of the day, but now I thought it was more like being completely overwhelmed by my own material. I perched on the edge of the stylishly cracked leather sofa and closed my eyes. I imagined my jaw sockets turning counterclockwise, unscrewing tension. My previous dentist was bucktoothed and beady-eyed, with a damp war-ren in the basement of a head shop in Fremont, but now a synthetic-haired young hygienist appeared as if to guide me on my spiritual journey. The examining cubes we passed had real walls instead of partitions, and each one, I noticed, was lined up with a window, so that you could float among Seattle's towers, enjoy composed angles onto Elliott Bay, and classical music. Here you are, said the hygienist, letting me go ahead. Just as I sank into the recliner, *Bachianas Brasileiras* gave chase over the ceiling-mounted speakers.

Eight cellos chewing up the scenery, I said, and the girl laughed uncertainly. I hauled in as much air as I could. I sighed it out again.

So, was I controlled or exposed? What was my position? I imagined Mosie with her dog pack. Her flabby flanks and hunched shoulders; the culty, closed sign language she used with the animals—

The hygienist was looking over the intake forms, her slender back turned against me. I couldn't help thinking she was Mosie's age. But I didn't think she lived in Shoreline in canine squalor.

It looks like you haven't filled out the medical history section, she said, still reading as she turned in her white medi-clogs. Could you do that for me?

I knew it was coming. My tears were cement in my throat. No, I thought to myself. No way I was going to check forty-five boxes. I took a deep breath and pictured myself filling with power.

The hygienist was staring curiously.

You know what? I said, sounding false, hopelessly strained, shaking my head too hard as cover. I can't do it.

Well, my goodness! said the hygienist. We have to know—

I cut her off. No heart murmur.

She thrust the clipboard at me, but I didn't take it. There was an almost earsplitting silence. A pure, ringing-with-cold silence, and I thought once again of Antarctica. So this was the new, non-babbling Sheila.

Oh, fine! I cried. A terrible keening sound came out of me. And then—uncontrolled, exposed—I could no longer stop myself from crying. Tears streamed as I tucked my head and carved a line down through all the No boxes. Of course I suffered headaches, hives, herpes. Anemia, anxiety, excessive thirst, but these were the secrets that made me who I was, and I wasn't going to give them away to any old dentist.

I handed back the clipboard. I was wretched. That's better, said the hygienist. I looked up into her eyes, the lashes cluttered and frozen with black makeup. Is that all you can open? I nodded. Everything she said, with her ice pick and her tiny mirror on a wand and her rinse gun in my mouth, I agreed with. The pick scraped the lime scale, punctured my gums, and my eyes watered, but I made myself as accepting as possible.

I walked past one of Stuber's pay lots farther up Second Avenue. I would shop until I was no longer in danger of crying. My mother would have done the same at the new dentist. Tried to assert herself, only to face humiliation. Maureen would have shopped until she was clear of crying. I was, in fact, so much like my mother that there was no need for me to have been born. No need for my mother to have died, was more like it.

Where did you come from, Mosie?

The doors of Nordstrom Rack split and sucked me in. I plunged my hands into the first exhibit I came to, pawed furiously through the dollar panties table, unburying X-rated thongs and days of the week in Necco Wafer colors.

Time seemed to turn me over, too, and I thought of my grandmother's things, as my mother called underwear, stashed underneath that rock, just in time for the crowning. The unpainted wood homestead reintegrated by the prairie. The light swam across the huge sky—there was so much light you could see clear through yourself, my mother once told me—and I saw myself—it shocked me—I was no longer a child.

STAND OF THE TIDE

My sister-in-law was carving her toenails over our bathtub. She must have opened the shade to get better light on the enterprise. I was crouched in the gutter along the side of the house where unchecked ivy was reconstituting the brick foundation into neatly sifted mounds of cayenne. She was a runner, a warrior, her feet clubbed and battered, but she thought she was safe inside. She was so absorbed that she didn't see me caught in my own frame, powder on my hands.

All weekend I'd been shooting off contempt for their cautious, late-in-life parenting style. It was as if I were determined to show them that they were more conventional than I, the younger sister whose kids had been raised by wolves—

A lone wolf, she-wolf, that was me.

Hey, I kept waving, over here! My Angie, her doctoral work on matrilinearity, a new literary form, and Rory, my high school dropout, director of documentary films, wow, me! My sister and sister-in-law's Petunia was three years old. That's what I called him. His name was Nashville. They'd both nursed him. They'd wanted Tennessee, but what if the playwright wasn't a feminist?

I'd had a dream, I said to the dinner table at large, where in a rising-tide situation, it was obvious that men and boys were of greater value and must be prioritized. The dream supplied life preservers and inflatable canoes.

But Petunia had not agreed to seafood, and my sisters were going to keep him in the dark about ketchup at least until he turned four. He made his horse rear—his high chair—

In unison, Oh, Nash!

I might have been watching my sister-in-law through the sights of a gun. I felt for a moment the all-consuming pause, as if the earth held back its tides, held perfectly still. What if all the Lee Harvey Oswalds, Mark David Chapmans, had been female? What if those loners, school shooters, disaffected youth back to Columbine, were girls?

I reversed course, backed carefully away from the window of my own house, letting my sister-in-law's body be.

CARTE BLANCHE

Dusk was a net and Hope fell through it, landing softly enough on lower Sixth Avenue. Storefronts gleamed like cleavers, the city serialized by materialism—a turn of phrase she could try out on her therapist. Tall and spare, she shrank out of the way of a couple of barrel-bodied policewomen.

There was a tumbling in her inner ear and her extremities tingled. Dry Eye Relief, read a little box half crushed in the gutter. So this was grief—as soon as she fought it off it swept back over her. A tide on a short cycle. In it came—Freddie— and out—had just left her.

She'd heard her mother's friends describe how they knew they had cancer before their diagnoses. Not the lumps in the shower, the doleful self-palpating, but the dogs who veered toward them on the street, sniffing urgently. Was there a black Lab in a service vest, swaybacked as an old bull, who could identify heartbreak? Who would dial yellow-brown eyes up to its mistress to signal that the trail of love had gone cold?

An African guy was coming toward her. It was just the two of them, New York's finest had vanished. He was short, compact, round-faced, his mind on his business. The forest people, Freddie would say dismissively. When Freddie shook himself out to his full height—

The Guinean passed in a thrum of incense and Hope wasn't sure she could walk any farther. Love had nothing to lose: it should, on principle, work out for everyone. In theory, love was a win-win situation. In reality she was at a total loss. She'd lost Freddie.

Kohl's, Old Navy, Filene's Basement birdcaged in scaffolding. Someone was doing crunches on a raft of cardboard.

She'd been inside this exact Duane Reade with Freddie. You a rich daddy girl, you never had one big toothbrush? he'd laughed, reaching for a tricked-out pedestal and charger.

She'd better pick up the pace. She hated to give her therapist anything to use against her. She'd find him sitting with his palms upturned on a small cushion on his lap. He flipped them impassively, at intervals, like cooking tofu.

A bath store had evidently jerry-rigged a fog machine for mango-papaya cartridges.

An uncomplaining, sidewalk-compliant sandwich board, three men's suits for ninety-nine dollars. She put her hands in her pockets to avoid the flier, and there was the reassuring totem of a tampon. Her therapist's clients were mostly women. She imagined the alpha girl who was the origin of all her periods. Her therapist himself was on a female moon cycle: he gave PMS as good as he got it.

Two years ago she'd strode in waving the Questionnaire to Determine Matrimonial Validity.

WHAT KIND OF WORK YOU DO?

HOW MUCH YOU EARN?

IS THAT RING INSCRIBED?

TELL ME YOU HUSBAND WIFE WARDROBE?

Her therapist had made a show of squinting when she produced a picture of Freddie in a blinding white T-shirt, straight from the package.

There was a chemical that flooded the brain like liquid amber to seal in desire. It hardened around traumas like love. It turned them into jewels you couldn't part with. She was full of stolen diamonds. She had sung soulful "Kumbaya/Come by Here's" at all-white summer camps. L'histoire d'une white girl, in the blond sun of a '70s Polaroid, she was pulling a red wagon, her hair a halo of birthday candles.

In seventh grade she'd stretched out, her center of gravity moved up to her throat, and when she became captain of the middle-school girls' volleyball team, her father informed her that Black guys were off limits. Let them be basketball stars, he said, football scholarships. Even comedians. He paused. But not—Dad! she stopped him. Or did she? In the privacy of their own Center Hall Colonial—the present cul-de-sac had been farmland—he could say what he pleased, couldn't he? Did he need to remind her it was a free country? The second-guessing of unstable liberals would tip the country right over. Every statistic was a sob story to the Democrats. They heaped federal funding on every single-mother cliché they ever met, not a crust of bread they couldn't turn into milquetoast. He ran his hands through his hair to give himself time to assess whether his joke had connected. The automatic ignition switch on the grill was acting up again—Bastard. Hope, he said, grab me the lighter. She swallowed elaborately, tracheally, like a heron. She had to use her wing to prop herself against the deck railing. Her father snorted and picked up the grill fangs. Each steak was topped with a pat of butter and a mineral flake of blue cheese he had prepped and portioned before getting loaded.

She'd basically majored in therapy. Upon graduation, a West Village walk-up had presented itself. Her father taped a ribbon across the threshold, but then his bashfulness gave way to bluster, and he marched in ahead of her. Her mother's eyes darted between three squares of view on brick and one on ailanthus. Later they'd met a tiny dog with a silver pigtail riding up the stairs in its mother's arms, which Hope's mother found reassuring.

A guy with the primate look of being shorter than his wife passed her. As if he personally were doing the work of challenging patriarchal norms and biases.

A redhead with soapy skin, perfect ringlets was humping the arm of her impassive nanny.

Hope felt herself detaching, drifting again, looking down on the sidewalk—

Avec degree she'd found a restaurant job where she met Alison, best friend at first sight, one blue eye like a sheepdog, a real poet of the people. Eagerly Hope had invited her to move in, but Alison pointed out that while she was waiting tables in diner towns in eastern Pennsylvania, Hope had barely registered the work-study hairnets who triaged the salad bar in her college cafeteria. Point taken. Was the only way to win Alison over to fall in love with her? On the brink of a consummative effort, Hope decided she was drawn to Alison's breasts because she had never breastfed. Alison touched her face: Poor baby. Thus, they became partners in the crime of arrested development—the West Village their Neverland, they were all in the spirit of pointy feathered hats, boots like long hooves, veggie-green tunics. They skipped past brightly colored mounds of fruit, stippled under the awning's shadow, a cross-dresser with grass hair, a velvet-lined trumpet case filled with pamphlets on the Second Coming, bridges like giant hammocks. Everywhere the smell of sugared cashews and incense. Their first boss, a hopelessly generous, alcoholic restaurant owner, would have staked them if they wanted to open their own bistro, but all they needed was the baguette that came back to the kitchen in napkined baskets, they could live on cinnamon toast, and French toast, and toast pizza.

Her thirtieth birthday was 9/11. Luckily she'd partied the night before, the end of an era. She sent the boy in her bed out into the ash storm. When next she checked she was thirty-one, a hardened character, a pragmatic cynic, like cubic zirconium. Regarding marriage, you couldn't be the center of your own life: you gave up the center of your bed and suddenly there was a spine down the mattress. As you got older together, doubling your oldness, you'd be obligated to contribute to the knee-jerk niggling, public and private, regarding your spouse's short-comings, a spastic picking at one another, a duet in Tourette's syndrome.

All of a sudden, she was not only an atheist of marriage but of everything. The fact that the superintendent of her building was a former Soviet bloc assassin with a lumpy mug like a walnut muffin. Leopards make love a hundred times in three days during the mating period, a mother millipede poops on her eggs to deter predators.

What are you trying to say? said Alison.

She was an atheist of time but it wasn't reciprocal. Time believed in Hope. Alison lifted a hank of hair to show her the cache of gray underneath—it looked oddly slick, and Hope felt herself retreat from Alison.

A young dad was determined to keep jogging behind the jogging stroller and Hope jumped out of the way. What is your problem, she said under her breath. Her limbs felt light for a moment. Her adrenaline was in gas form, the last of the moisture in her body.

A family of French tourists beheld the Chrysler Building as the daylight shuttered down around them. She kept walking.

Their next restaurant was tucked backward on one of those Village streets that seemed counterclockwise, the whole neighborhood in violation of the street grid. Velvet curtains suggested the den of a ten-dollar palm reader, and floor staff wore fitted vests, long aprons that flattered the wasp-waisted busboys, a lineage of Bangladeshis majoring in business. They talked fast, among themselves, as if they were one body, and she had asked once if they had all known each other in Bangladesh. Kiran curled his lip. Then eyed her up and down owningly.

Well into the doldrums of a Tuesday evening, the door jingled and all roused in time to behold a full-length black fox angle inside from behind the curtains. He flicked his skinny head around and a deep voice, almost a ventriloquism, emanated.

Hope felt Kiran nudge her forward.

Just pull it over my head, said the slight human in rippling fur, both imposing and impatient. He regarded Hope without blinking, and without making a move to unwrap himself, so that she was compelled to register first his dyed-to-match black hair, and then the fact that the sleeves of the coat hung empty.

As soon as she'd turned the cascade of fur over to the coat check, their hollow-cheeked, table-for-one was striding into the depths of her unpopulated section.

A scourge of PETAs, he declared, sliding into the booth. Fortunately, the good constable arrived and a bloodbath on the temple stairs was averted. He sighed. The temple known as Bloomie's. Bring me a glass of Burgundy.

When Hope returned with the wine and a basket of bread she saw that the table caught him at the breastbone. Before she could worry, he stretched his neck, and with the spade of his chin drew the basket closer. He was wearing a touch of lipstick. Nodding approval, he engaged in a quick costume change under the table and a few seconds later passéd one naked, slender, bone-white foot up to rest delicately to the right of his place setting. He pointed it like a dancer. Fillet of sole, he said. You're most welcome to watch my little freak show.

The six-ounce foot articulated and grasped the stem of the wineglass. He brought it to his lips, glancing at her from beneath his lashes. He uncurled his toes toe by toe to set the glass down again.

That's amazing, said Hope.

The following night she was off, but she stopped by at closing to regale Alison. From behind the bar, Alison passed her a giant sundae glass of that same Burgundy. What did he tell you?

Tell me? Her ready laugh flickered out uncertainly.

Alison was quiet, perhaps allowing it to hit her. How could she have been so insipid, uninspired?

She wandered into the kitchen to retrieve Alison's staff meal of Tabasco'ed penne with the side of pickle relish that was somehow called salad. How brightly lit and humid it was compared to the romantically dim and arid dining room. Post-dinner-rush beer bottles were stashed behind upended nylon cutting boards cilantro green in their grooves from thousands of garnishes; the hostess, a rawboned ballerina après grueling ronds de jambe and psychologically demeaning auditions, was spooning directly from the sorbet tub. The grease-splattered boom box did a bump-and-grind along the counter, the DJ driving one song off the embankment while the new song filled in from all directions. Around the corner half a dozen kitchen guys, aproned to their boots, had formed a dancing circle.

Hope stepped onto a rubber footstool to see better. Who was the Black guy in the center? He was taller than the others, seemingly in a state of hypnotic self-absorption, coiling and uncoiling. Priestly as well as princely, at once vain and unguarded. Her breathing was shallow. She stumbled off the stool and backed out of the steamy kitchen.

Alison still had customers. Two regulars in thin dress shirts who lived in the building, and the Pen Man, in the corner, in his Depression-era overcoat with a suitcase full of ballpoints—at least he had the historical dignity of the traveling salesman. Hope slipped behind the bar to help Alison polish glasses.

Last call, Alison said mildly to the regulars. In the glassy bar light her head was the color of tarnished silver. The front door jingled and echoed from the empty, tiled dining room.

Alison glanced irritably at her bunch of keys. She hadn't locked up yet. She gave a short sigh and kept counting. Grimly she folded and stapled little cash packages.

The bar was cloaked off from the dining room, the kitchen doors were closed, plexi windows fogged over. All of a sudden someone had breached the bar area and he was oncoming, with a low swagger as if he were working his pants down toward his flat feet in broken sneakers. He wore bulbous muttonchops, like coalbin smudges, and before Hope could make any sense of it, he had squared off against Alison.

Look at the gut on you, said Alison.

Hope had the strange feeling that Alison was continuing a conversation of yesterday, and all the yesterdays before it.

The intruder grinned, molesting his stomach. His hair was yarn and his eyes bloodshot. Was Hope in a movie? A no-budget student film? She'd dated one of those guys, in the *Blair Witch* era. He'd always seemed to be herding a preschool of equipment.

You kids have some cash on you?

And just like that, Hope had her first-ever gun drawn and pointed. Almost simultaneously, the tall dark African glided out of the kitchen.

There was no real way to avoid midtown without going so far east or west that the air was thinner. Hope was forced to slow with the crowd. Always some bike-messenger-type scalloping into the street to pass, then getting stuck at the same cross street as mere mortals, lifting his haunches off the seat, balancing standing on the pedals. Genital-ware exposed, shouldn't it have been men who rode sidesaddle?

On the other side of the glass wall of a shoe store, a white woman held up a mule for inspection. There was swelling around her eyebrows and her ankles were purplish, like an ostrich's. Freddie with his Michael Jordan kicks, Michael Jackson slippers, single-use Payless knockoffs. Why you don't have more heel, Baby?

She cleared Rockefeller Center.

The air was cleaner uptown, like it had been Windexed. The buildings darker, holograms with no referents, a long rectangle of traffic cut and pasted from a movie—

She felt as if she were on some goat trail far below.

She had watched Freddie pull into himself, gathering his forces. Then his arm snapped the air like a whip and struck the gun from the hand of the dirtbag. That was all it took. The stickup was over.

The Guatemalans bayed and patted their own weapons in their Timberlands and shooed Freddie off his shift like aunties. Hope couldn't stop shaking and laughing convulsively. It was as if just seeing a gun would do her this great injury.

Alison kept saying *shit*, and after a while the repetition was obvious. This word is not a girl, said Freddie, and Hope laughed with him, and warming up, he bowed to Alison. You think I'm a funny guy? His voice was deep and it rattled. Alison motioned for him to sit and he leaned against the bar as Hope undid her hair so that it filled in the space between her jaw and shoulders. Very classical, said Freddie, and before Hope's eyes were the lions and zebras of his trompe l'oeil accent. Cote d'Ivoire, he told them, and Hope saw a pack of moons, a loose-jointed Land Rover, an incinerating sunset.

Now why you two girls not marry? said Freddie. And he was looking right at her.

What was her problem? But if she had ever felt what she felt now—spaciousness, an outer space of singing stars—

Well Freddie, said Alison, and Hope suddenly wished Alison wouldn't mock him. That criminal you drove off? Alison answered herself, Turns out, that was my very own ex-husband.

It took Hope a moment. Alison still had to break down her bar and she turned her back on them.

Hours after she'd tucked herself into her loft bed she was still awake, alternately riled up, post-traumatic, then combing through the long strange evening. The way she and Alison being single had seemed, before tonight, inviolable. The way she and Freddie had left the restaurant together— the web of Village streets in concentric circles, hot swamp through the subway grates, silt in the gutters, garbage trucks and taxis catapulting down the oil-slick avenue. I'll see you again? he'd asked her, and she was floating up there where the office buildings had greenish windows like wraparound sunglasses.

It dawned on her that her whole life up to now had been in this unserious, ironic register, and careless of its own pacing. She imagined Freddie standing alone on the subway platform, listening to the harmonics of tracks answering other tracks, the scuffle of rats, and the wet snore coming from a side of cardboard. A train to Queens at three in the morning?

*

Almost without missing a beat, he said he knew a Dominican lawyer who specialized in Green Cards. Cousin Jacques paid two thousand dollars to a Dominican girl who got her citizenship from a cousin to whom she had paid fifteen hundred. So! said Freddie triumphantly, his hands around Hope's naked waist. Easy!

They squeezed down a Styrofoam hallway above a Chinese restaurant that smelled like green beans, instant ramen. Freddie packed his cigarettes with a thwack against his giant palm. The door to the lawyer's office was behind a flap, a dilapidated drawbridge of brown carpet. Freddie raised his fist as in a propaganda poster, a guerilla in a police state with a one-product economy, ivory, gold, emigrants—and knocked for both of them. Hope tried to pinch in closer, but her groom took one determined and obvious step so that he entered the office before her. Only to mumble, I have your reference of Jacques—

You want to pay now or yesterday? said the lawyer.

Freddie's eyes narrowed. The lawyer pumped out exactly three units of laughter. He smacked the desk. They were to lay their hearts right there without further demonstration. They remained standing. The lawyer shrugged. They could stand all day. Mr. Africa, he began. You can read English?

I have post-baccalaureate engineerical degree in aeronautics of my country university, said Freddie.

UTILITY BILLS SHOULD BE IN BOTH? read the lawyer. PROVIDE OF NAMES, AGES COUPLE'S BROTHERS AND SISTERS, THE AUNTS AND UNCLES? CURRENT PLACE OF RESIDENCE AND HOW LONG YOU HAVE LIVED IN THERE? The lawyer looked out over the top of his reading glasses, To give you a coupla situation.

He held it out, the Questionnaire to Determine Matrimonial Validity, twenty-eight pages xeroxed on hot-pink paper. Hope could see him taking a female underling out for lychee fruit in order to get her to correct the spelling. WRITE YOU REAL NAME AND COMPLETELY NAME, ALSO ANY NAME YOU KNOWN BY, INCLUDE ALIASES.

AGE AT TIME YOU ARE MEETING?

Hope Hardy, thirty-two, F. A. Koné, twenty-five—I'm a little boy compare of you, Baby, grinned Freddie.

WHAT IS THE NAME OF FUNCTIONAR (MINISTER THAT FORMALIZE YOU MARRIAGE) AND WHO HIRE HIM?

Freddie looked at her and her heart swelled although she knew no ministers. She lost herself for a moment in the shine of the plate of his forehead, his shirt like silky water, the surprisingly rough skin underneath it.

Get your stories straight, couple, said the lawyer. Freddie set his jaw. His confidence seemed so pure. And also immature, a provision of his ego.

GIVE SOME OF YOUR NEIGHBORS DATA, barked the lawyer.

Freddie lowered his voice: Chérie, is better I stay at your place. It took her breath away. She saw them doing the questionnaire together like a crossword. Cut to: her grandchildren, those gentle mochas of a broad-minded future, eagerly waiting at her feet for her to fix their hair in cornrows—

The lawyer lit an air cigar, put his feet up. They know white people don't talk to the neighbors.

Hope's descendants scattered like earth-toned children in an urban-renewal wall mural. Freddie coughed into the horn of his hand. Please, he said thickly. Hope is friend to all people.

DO YOU RECEIVE FINANCIAL AID FROM YOUR COUPLE HOW OFTEN? She saw Freddie's long lazy form down her bed like the shadow of a melting snow angel. His big clothes draped over the chair in the corner, below them, enormous blue jeans, enormous pullover. All brand-name clothing. Just then a girl with high-gloss beige tips and embellished hair poked her head in. She was holding out the change, in cash, for the half hour. Freddie reached for it.

That's mine, Hope heard herself saying, and the girl widened her eyes and retracted the five dollars. Hope felt tears welling.

Little lady, clicked the lawyer.

Outside, night had fallen. Nurses clumped, smoking, by the back entrance of a hospital. A dumpster banged, a lowrider with its metal skirt pulled all the way down over its wheels throbbed by. The streetlights seemed to buzz in answer.

He must feel powerless, she told herself, with her holding all the cards. The carte blanche and the green one.

He had to wait for her as she fumbled with the door of her building—the lock was piss-sticky. One of her neighbors was coming out and Freddie stepped back to let him pass. Thanks man, said the neighbor.

She could feel the weight of Freddie shaking his head behind her when she couldn't open the door of her apartment either. Hope, he said, I can help you. Once more, her throat closed around tears.

You have one big race problem in your country, he observed, reaching for his T-shirt. She lay outside the sheets, gray from his body dandruff. They had hardly finished making love. He wouldn't wear a condom. It's not a guy's problem, he insisted, and she could see how it sort of wasn't.

There's too much—he paused, snapping his fingers to try to scare up the word in English, giving up—émotion.

Hope sat up beside him. She drew her knees in. He pushed them down again, first one, then the other. You think you have some Black lover for rédemption, he said thoughtfully. I think I have this white girl so I get my Green Card. And then suddenly laughing, poking, tickling, he took her in his arms again.

Alison blew in late for her shift, waving her work shirt around by the hanger. She'd been detained, she said, on Knickerbocker, just blocks from her apartment, two cop cars pulling some kind of playbook formation. This was a fucked-up city, Brooklyn in particular disgusted her, she was ditching her apartment with its railroad rooms, hot-tar roof looking down on laundry ladders, beefcake tomcats, unspayed females, soundtrack of ambulances from the ER bay across the street, useless L train. She looked around acidly. Did anyone want it?

Do you have to have a car out there? a new waitress ventured. Server. Alison didn't deign to answer.

Then she lunged at the girl, Guns drawn! My brake light is out, which automatically makes it a stolen vehicle.

A few kitchen guys were listening. You white, Miss. What you care? The new dishwasher was freckle-faced but serious.

Intimidation is not okay, said Alison, channeling, despite herself, the new lingo. Why can't men keep anything in their trousers?

The kitchen guys laughed. They trying to protect you, said the dishwasher, Eduardo. He was gathering an audience. From guys like us who steal cars, Miss.

My neighbor Lina is beating her four children with non-stick cookware, said Alison.

Hope said, Are you going to call or something?

Miss Alison she need a more love life, said Ricky at the salad station. Eduardo my cousin he available.

When Hope landed at the bar at the end of night, Alison turned on her, Hey, old pal. We should hang out some time. Hope froze and Alison relented, What's Freddie up to lately?

Just that morning, Hope had watched him drop another pair of white sports socks into the trash from his six feet six inches. The heels were stained caramel like campfire marshmallows. If you knew your couple disposed of his sports socks after one use, would you still love him? If he could not afford to buy new socks? If you bought him socks yourself so he would mourn at home on his days off and maybe your face would supplant dreams of his mother in her headdress?

I am stuck here in a rat race, said Freddie, echoing the university students who milled around his cousin Jacques's incense blanket. Beads, batiks, djembe drums like orphaned saints, skunk-striped ebonywood carvings. It is not human to work all the time like this, he argued in his light French, his Gauguin, over his Marlboro breakfast. He took his cheap-looking expensive sunglasses from his Hawaiian shirt and lowered his face behind them incredulously, Everybody go to université but not for working.

Chérie-baby, said Freddie. Come to this party of my people. They entered through a trapdoor in a sidewalk. Five hundred Africans in a Harlem basement two blocks square drinking hibiscus juice at room temperature, sharing weed, drummers with impossibly small waists in multicolored diaper pants, beautiful muscular women in full regalia cooking whole fish in a firepit.

Freddie wore a Kangol. Hope had caught him pressed into the mirror, eyeliner pencil raised. She didn't mean to shame him but the spectacle had shocked her. Then it worked its way under her skin and aroused her.

He checked on her at intervals. Dancing is for me everything, he said, punching her upper arm lightly. He twisted back into the crowd, his head loose on its neck, arms folded in against the instrument of his torso, then flung high, fingers in fringes. Babies as big as grown men breathed down Hope's breasts where she sat on a stool she was using as a mooring.

She saw one other white girl, who she mistook at first for a world music album cover—heartily embroidered circle skirt, Converse spats, fat gray dreads like sexual appendages. She was smoking a pipe witchily. It wasn't all that different from college, thought Hope, the low-ceilinged living room of a North Benn party house, blackout curtains, sourdough couches pushed up against the walls. She could still feel the scrape of salt crystals and loose gravel underfoot in winter, taste the alloy of alcohols bonded to promote date rape. Her dimwitted heart, fuzzy for rescue. Even so, she had to admit that her world and Freddie's were unyieldingly separate, and that any meeting in the middle, any merging, was so deeply personal as to leave no public record.

The witchy girl was making her way over. Up close, she was younger than Hope, but wiser. Hope scaled herself down in submission. She didn't have to be told she'd strayed into someone else's territory. The dreadlocks were long moldy cocoons, painful-looking bare skull between them. Hope sensed the kind of feminism expressed in a controlling individuality. A dogmatic suspicion toward both women and men.

Hey girl, she said without smiling. You here with somebody?

I am. Hope tried to sound neither appeasing nor provoking.

The girl stretched her mouth to grin but her eyes were hard. You're not big into dancing? Which is okay, she went on, cause they don't like their main lady to be dancing.

Oh, Hope laughed.

The girl appeared to survey the scene. Hope felt nothing in common with her. Not whiteness, not gender. Someone blew a head of smoke between them. Contact high, said Hope.

Don't smoke that shit, the girl said flatly.

No, I actually wouldn't.

Hey. We just met but I feel like I've known you forever. Did the girl think showing her teeth passed for a smile? You could say there's a whole class of white girls with vaginas like Green Cards, she continued. You know you can never get close to them. Welcome to your latent racism. It's not about your guilt, it's not about the Middle Passage. She paused. It's biotribal. I should have been an anthropologist. She turned her full-power gaze on Hope. It's nothing to be ashamed of.

Hope laughed again. Can I disagree with you?

Oh girl.

Which one is yours? Hope caught herself gesturing a little wildly at the dancers.

The girl laughed harshly. You got *that* right. I'm four and a half months pregnant.

At that moment Freddie swept their way, eyeing the girl with displeasure, and Hope found herself pulling away from him when he reached for her. The girl stuck out her bottom lip, looking them over. Hope saw now that she was ugly, an empty little pouch for a chin.

You ready to go home, Baby? said Freddie.

Yes, breathed Hope, only then giving herself over.

A cab was a fortune from such an outpost, and Hope, still unnerved, didn't offer. Freddie ushered her through the subway station with its sobering, musty chill, and for a moment she was seized by fear of the crypt and she clung to him. Concrete staircases with no outlets, platforms and balconies like calcified cumulus, rats the size of raccoons—or shrunken humans. Trains would be sparse at this hour.

Suddenly Freddie was talking to someone on a balcony above them. Hope followed his gaze upward: a girl wrapped, double wrapped in a long black cape coat, crying and throwing things out of her handbag. Her face against the coat was whiter than Hope's. Now Hope could hear her sobs between the echoey, nightbird sounds of the station. Who's that? she said.

She had to repeat herself.

The girl called down, Haven't you heard of Katya?

It's just a Polish girl who used to let me stay at her place, said Freddie.

Does she need help? said Hope.

Yeah, the mental help. Freddie tapped his head. Go home, he called up at her. A quarter hit his forehead. It bounced to the floor and he kicked it into the train bed. He took Hope's elbow.

Out on the street, Freddie looked through the solid dark blocks of buildings. He began to sing softly in Hope's ear and she curled into him. Suddenly she felt her love for Freddie was multiplied by the love of the girl with the deceased dreadlocks, and by the love of this Katya, as if she, Hope, had to bear their pain in love as well as her own. Her love was all love, universal.

It was the kind of spring night that dabbled in heretofore wintered corners. There was a smell like wet gravestones, warm air layered with cold air like sediment. She held him back when a pigeon, green and purple, uselessly fancy, dropped in their path and futzed for a flap of ham on the sidewalk. Magnanimously she granted the bird's right to place a lavender claw on the meat before she moved in on it.

Chérie, you have cash for a taxi?

YOU HAVE A KEY TO THE POSTAL BOX? (SHOW IT)

YOU DATE OTHER BEFORE EACH MARRIAGE? WHERE YOU GO HOW MANY?

She was tied in skeins of sheet in the loft bed. The pillows were flattened. Freddie was performing his toilette after lovemaking. Fifteen minutes of loofah, fifteen minutes of baby oil, then cold, then soap. She could hear all the water running, the sink, the shower, the toilet.

What do you think, shot Freddie, coming out in a towel. I never had a girl before you?

Who pinched your earlobe with her tiny yellow teeth, seed beads, her voice picking the strings of the idiosyncratic dialect? When Hope learned a word of it by accident, Freddie acted as though she'd blasphemed the Koran, which he blasphemed regularly.

Hope heard herself saying what Freddie always said, You don't understand anything. Love. She ran hot water in the kitchen sink—her whole inventory of glasses had been used once and left for dirty. One by one she filled them with soap suds. She had to find a washcloth to dry them. Freddie had a habit of using her dish towels to wipe his face after he went running with Jacques or one of the other West Africans. I don't run with girls, he told her, offended, when she asked to join him.

*

She glanced at herself as she hustled past plate glass. Nearly six feet tall herself, and caved in the middle like Kokopelli. Wouldn't you think you could manage to fix just one thing about yourself by now, Hope Hardy?

A quick check at the next cross street. She was going to be even later for her therapist than she'd projected. It was likely he would never say anything she didn't know already. Extremely probable he was not a bearer of meaning.

A mere boy in chef's whites switchbacked downstream, swinging last-minute bodega groceries.

Another Duane Reade. The automatic doors had been jammed open and they hummed in helpless consternation.

The sidewalk became a clearing. A bus pumped up behind her. Mica glittered on the ground.

The sky was as viscous as laundry detergent.

A flock of school kids in dark uniforms split and fractaled around her. For a moment, she was part of their pattern.

She was on a collision course with a fashionista whose hair floated above his cathedral. He passed straight through her. There was only a rush in her ears to let her know she among humans.

She tried teasing. What if I say we were married at three and you say four thirty, Freddie? They'll smell a rat, the Immigration folks? They'll be able to tell the love isn't quite authentic?

He pretended not to hear. She headbutted his stomach gently. It's not fair I have to memorize all eight of your sisters! Aminata, Berenice—she chanted.

Be serious.

It was Thanksgiving, the dull and crowded twenties of November. Apples, silver, damask, and those singleserve waters, sweating shyly, that lined her parents' refrigerator. At the very least, she and Freddie would rehydrate.

He's so dark I can't see his features, said her mother, when Freddie went outside for a cigarette. Is he handsome?

Do you remember that girl in your class in about the fifth grade, Hopester? said her father, at dinner. Chinese girl? Her parents had already put her to work in their stir-fry palace.

Why do white people feel compelled to gorge when they eat Asian? thought Hope suddenly. In his surprise, and then relief at not having to split his wine, her father was effusive. But wine is an emblem of our civilization, Freddie!

I'm so curious, said her mother. What do you think of our American Blacks, Freddie? We covered rap music with our lecture group, and it just seems so sad that their body of reference is so limited.

Freddie wasn't bothering to follow. Her mother wasn't important. Where was he? Among his multitude of brothers and sisters? Concrete floor, maafe, mango, poulet bicyclette, dogs, uncles, aunts as constant as the radio . . . Who was he? She loved him for his small eyes, his basketball-star arms, his clean feet, his tight hair like dry moss. Was it not conceivable that she and Freddie were old souls, social-emotional aboriginals, with the capacity to transcend race and culture?

The chin-up bar was still in the doorway of her girlhood bedroom. How had she failed to notice this all the years she'd come dutifully home for holidays? How had she forgotten the fan letters she'd written Nadia Comaneci? Freddie's knees almost touched the ground when he hung off the bar but he said with real amazement, Why we don't have this one in our apartment?

On Black Friday, she insisted on driving to a Christmas fair in a neighboring county. You're sexy when you drive, Chérie-Coco. He watched out the window of her mother's S-Class. Real America, he said with approval. She saw only a long, cab-less box truck mated primitively to a thin-ply metal warehouse.

Fried dough, apple strudel, turkey drumsticks, half-mile turkey sausage. I love this place! cried Freddie, throwing his chest out. New York is one shithole! He grabbed her tightly. You're beautiful, my girl. For once it was Hope who had to break free when her palm became intolerably sweaty. She glowed with pride. He was uncannily good at shooting an air rifle into a bank of stuffed animals.

We gonna make it, he whispered later, and she knew he was thinking about his Green Card, but he couldn't have been ignorant of the way it suggested something bigger.

A late streetlight stuttered to life. These evening sessions were extreme after daylight savings. Only in New York would a therapist be booked all day, when everyone everywhere else was working. A pair of chunky, blond teenagers wearing their small purses crosswise appeared lost, but excited.

She caught Freddie ashing absentmindedly on the questionnaire. All three of her ashtrays were in the sink, the butts soaked in Dr. Pepper, cylindrical little sponges. She slid the questionnaire out from underneath his elbow and put a saucer down beside him.

HAD YOU GIVE OR SEND PRESENTS?

A burgundy pleather jacket with belt and tail, oversize plastic buttons. She imagined the sidewalk sales in Chinatown: Timex, Rolex, Pucci, Gucci.

Back downtown from the lawyer's they exited the Four-teenth Street station at Twelfth Street and walked until they came to the promontory at Bleecker and Sixth Avenue, bode-ga to bodega, bisecting the Village, pizza, tacos, Father Demo Square plastered with pigeons.

He pulled her in, she folded along the vertical, she stum-bled against the hulls of his Timberlands.

I love you! she said into his own fake leather jacket.

Humor in his voice, but it was shared humor, Want to get married?

Her laughter originated way down in her uterine chakra, if there was one. Her stomach was blowing around as if it weren't an organ but a thistle.

A postal carrier in a smart skirt was unlocking a mailbox. A tiny old lady was peeing her pet underneath the permanent awning of her building's doorway. Was it a dog? They weren't going to get any farther. The old lady had shrunk inside her plaid wool overcoat. Hope could see the double-breasted doorman in the lobby, keeping an eye on them.

She didn't want to die of grief here on the sidewalk. Up Columbus now, through the dark particles.

I have no word for your eyes, Freddie said once, cobra-ed above her on the loft bed.

IF YOUR HUSBAND IS TRAVEL OUTSIDE OF USA, WHICH IS THE FREQUENCY YOU VISIT HIM AND WHAT WAS THAT YOU DID THERE?

Would you take me to far Afrique?

There are no convenience, he stated, thereby forbidding, but she thrilled to the matter of whether she'd go where you eat goat meat.

Maybe your eyes are sky? said Freddie. And there she was, stranded, cold, far above where their bodies lay, their magnets sucked to stars at opposite ends of some black, refrigerated universe.

DESCRIBE YOUR RESIDENCE FURNITURE?

HAD YOU RECENTLY BOUGHT A PIECE OF FURNITURE?

WHO SELL IT TO YOU?

HOW MUCH YOU PAY?

IS YOUR PLACE CARPETING?

DESCRIBE THE TV SET?

Post-coital stupor, arm like a pendulum over the side of the loft bed, he perused the questionnaire with catlike detachment. This thing is *shit*, isn't it. Carelessly he tossed it overboard. Even I know is not good English. He tested her out sideways. The pen had made little purple tattoos on the pillow.

DESCRIBE YOU'RE LOVE AFFAIR

EXAMLES ARE: AT FIRST SIGHT

ARRANGED OF RELATIONS

WORKING IN SIMLAR VLOCATION

PLEASE EXPLAIN THE OTHER

She stood before her therapist's building now. The sidewalk was just pixels. No doorman, a long list of brass nameplates, wallpaper that was supposed to look like an old-world map in the otherwise stingy foyer.

Everyone said there'd be a knock on the door at three a.m. and they'd better be snuggled in the same bed with the knowledge of the color of the other's toothbrush. The lawyer crooked his finger: With the names of aunties, uncles, and cousins. But the immigration agent was more like a social worker, long defeated, and he'd stopped by midmorning, carrying a cloth briefcase.

He'd accepted Hope's offer of coffee. A minute later she had to sheepishly amend it to tea. Freddie descended the loft bare chested.

She would have had his mysteries to herself, his treasures would have been her treasures. She would have had a claim on him. What came over her? At the finish line!

It was as if she couldn't leave her power alone. She had to corrupt it.

Her therapist startled. Had she finally caught his attention? The single window of his ground floor office faced the street but he never closed the blind. The bare glass was a dark mirror.

She'd called it off, canceled the green-card application. It was a test. Like in a fairy tale. Did he love her?

He went straight back to Katya.

Who? said her therapist. Hope was the last client of the day, forgive him if he was blanking. The Polish girl who'd rained coins on them, curses.

ROSE

In the first week of her first and only year of college, fresh-
men could orient with a hot air balloon. She signed herself up
for Introduction to Philosophy, because she lived
in her mind, and the professor was Greek, with a name
like a biblical era or an early goddess. He turned out to be
a small, tidy man with a debonair fealty to the material
and a materiality—as if they were handstitched leather, or bright hammered
coins—to his accented words. She'd been a remarkably early
reader but in adolescence had unlearned, and now it was clear
she had no business anywhere near the page.
She had a bike, and she rode around, very
sad. Her roommate was an innocent from deep-woods Maine
whose parents had obviously snatched her as
an infant, swapped out
their hairy little gizmo. Come to find out such
beauty and goodness could never be their own. When
her roommate changed clothes, her breasts looked like they were still growing.
It was hard not to stare. Doing her laundry

anguished the gulf but at least

she was using her hands. Boys showed interest and she lost her hair

on the shore of a lake with a feeling of ritual but no referent where

she established the underpinnings of a private

sophistry she went on to outline in her final paper for philosophy

describing the switch at birth

of her organs. She had a rose

where the rational should have been. She saw red, and her energy

was old. She set herself

on course for a life of prohibitions

and passions, the thorns of which bleed her still.

TIME OF THE TESTUDINIDAE

I don't have that kind of time.

I can't sit still in rooms.

No windows, bruised walls, a working team of four-year-olds drives the climbing structure around the waiting room, hand-holds like holes in Swiss cheese.

I'm racing inside.

"Barn door's open," says a dad to a lone loose-waisted boy watching daytime TV.

A slightly older boy with friar hair and huge hiking boots is dismissed from the inner rooms. In a starry voice, he quizzes the nurse holding the door, "What is the longitude and latitude of Providenciales, Turks and Caicos?"

"Homeschool," I whisper to my teenage son.

Time presses like a herd into my ear corral.

Finally, a nurse in patterned scrubs, pj's, calls us from a clip-board, carefully pronouncing our name. She fits into a second skin as I ascend the swing-arm throne. The needle makes a dent before it breaks blood, though I don't have much collagen anymore. Eyes trained on the vial as it's topped off, she says to my son, "You next, hon?"

I'm a disciple of common speech, but like the voice of God I can't replicate it. I run into her the next day at the supermarket, and we greet each other like old friends. Coincidence makes us believe in Providence.

*

The last consumer age was marked by the beginning of bookstores with Scotch-plaid armchairs, ladders on rails. A Borders flagshipped the Providence Place Mall, and young mothers like me released our babies down the aisles past cross-legged nannies employed by older moms.

A couple of artist-squatters fashioned a secret apartment in the hollow eaves above the mall parking garage. I was never there, but I know people who shared ramen with them. They used doll-size pots and bowls.

*

I cut through the pine grove in back of the high school. It's like a tide pool, a miniature but with real wind.

My mind is shallow water in the sun. The snails at the copper bottom are little giants.

I come across my best friend's house on Zillow. Dirty dishes in the sink, the medicine cabinet flung open, we haven't talked in three years. I'm breaking the rule, the fourth wall, not to write about real people. The work-around is that I'm writing about myself, like in the interpretation of dreams everyone is really you. Is her house my house? Is my house a train wreck?

*

I board the train just to sit still. It seems like it should take great effort to clear Providence, but in less than a minute, light flexing between brick mill buildings, the train glides behind Home Depot.

South Attleboro, a shopping cart straddles the embankment; Mansfield, dominoes of helium graffiti; Canton Junction, a badly stained river forgotten by all but teenagers. We sweep past a snow farm, dirt-battered berms and hillocks unmoved by April's cold rain.

Hyde Park, Ruggles, Back Bay.

I won't Google the city map when I emerge. Why do I continue to capitalize Google and God? Somewhere along the line I got old for my age, complaining about not being able to write freely anymore for fear of making type-size faces out of semicolons and parentheses.

My mother complains that older women have degraded fingerprints. Unlocking her phone has become difficult. In her time, feminism meant unpainted toenails. In mine, it means having time for a pedicure. I don't have that kind of time.

*

My customer service representative, stagehand to technology, speaks English down a narrow stone passage. "Romania!" I echo. I see a stock-image Gare du Nord, long tables provisionally laid with monitors and headsets, cords everywhere, no enamel on old teeth or old toilets.

"You've been in the news over here a lot lately," I say.

He laughs gamely, and I see an ambitious young man in unwashed jeans, worrying his Saint Christopher medal. "If you're speaking of the Syrians," he says, "there is nothing for them here."

"Oh!" I'm suddenly self-conscious. Syrians in unadapted windbreakers, track pants, boats like old technology, they can't swim.

It takes almost three hours to install Microsoft Word. "Until now I've had the luck of walking outside to a light rain," he says in parting, and I take this to mean that tonight it's pouring in Romania, the black cobbled streets outside the train station runneling like many rivers to the sea.

*

Is it worse to care and do nothing, or not to care? I'm all set up with the Excel-PowerPoint-Word package. Worse for whom?

The drama of the tortoise has to do with longevity and lack of speed.

The human drama is the fact that we're all refugees from death.

Garden of End Times behind the fencing club in East Providence. Or is it the beginning? I'm like a tribeswoman with mange and beads, or Mitochondrial Eve, pacing Eden, trying to get hungry. New ditches, new kudzu, knotweed in the slicked-back soil. Portuguese names for empty industrial cul-de-sacs that back up on back lots of car dealerships below 195; my sons inside the warehouse, slashing saber and foil. The road is scourged with greasy potholes. My hems are getting heavy, and I bend down to roll up my jeans.

The whole story seizes in vestigial surprise.

It's hard to get the drama right, the timing, in the telling here, but one more step and I'd trip over a commando-style tortoise in the middle of the road. And it seems tricky, upside-down, to say I'm scared of a creature so drastically downscaled in the Anthropocene, but I suddenly feel naked before God. Cauldron shell, cast bronze caked with mud. Small eyes poked into gritty head-flesh, its beak is mean. Folds of ancient tapestry hang off its hind legs, toenails like pine cones, and as if it finally feels me staring, it bends its knees in slow motion, drops its vertebral tail, and sinks deeply into its form.

Tortoise time passes.

Time tilts—

downward. Years go by. The tortoise labors to a start, stumbling over ruts as if its legs were nerveless, bearing its ancestors' terrain.

ACKNOWLEDGMENTS

Many thanks to the editors of the literary magazines where some of these stories first appeared, sometimes in different versions: "The Sea" (as "Marie and Roland") in *Lady Churchill's Rosebud Wristlet*, "Ambush" in *The Southern Review*, "Double-Check for Sleeping Children" and "Soldier" in *AGNI*, "Naiad" in *the Laurel Review*, "First Love" in *Vestal Review*, "Inheritance" in *New England Review*, "Stop In For A Free Coffee If You're From Arkansas" in *New Delta Review*, "Twelfth Night" in *Alaska Quarterly Review*, "V-J Day" in *Joyland*, "A Seduced World" in *Epiphany*, "Janus" (as "When We Were Interesting") in *Juked*, "Mother's Helper" in *The Hopkins Review*, "Uncollected Territories" in *The Common*, "Stand of the Tide" in *The Florida Review*, and "Time of the Testudinidae" in *American Short Fiction*, where it was the 2019 winner of the *American Short Fiction* Prize, chosen by Danielle Dutton. Thank you to Natasha Le Bel for the line "a passionate claustrophobia," which I borrowed from her poem "Boxing the Female" for my story "Great Cathedrals." Adrienne Rich chose the poem, which Le Bel wrote at seventeen, for the wonderfully contentious, visionary 1996 *Best American Poetry*. Finally, I'm especially and deeply grateful to Bill Pierce, Jen Acker, Carolyn Kuebler, Phoebe Oathout, Diane Josefowicz, and Michael Allio for working through these stories with extraordinary skill, generosity, and grace.